DOMINANT TRAITS

STORIES
BY ERIC FREEZE

DUFOUR EDITIONS

First published in the United States of America, 2012
by Dufour Editions Inc., Chester Springs, Pennsylvania 19425

ISBN 978-0-8023-1350-8

Cover Photo: © Julija Sapic | Dreamstime.com

Library of Congress Cataloging-in-Publication Data

Freeze, Eric, 1974-
  Dominant traits : stories / by Eric Freeze.
    p. cm.
  Includes bibliographical references and index.
  ISBN 978-0-8023-1350-8 (pbk. : alk. paper)
  I. Title.
  PR9199.4.F7375D66 2012
  813'.6--dc23

                                        2011043005

Printed and bound in the United States of America

For Rixa

Contents

WRONG TIME FOR CAUTION

The gas station where I work is a 7-11 that sells Slurpees even in the middle of January, which, if you don't know Crowsnest, can be cold, 60 below with the wind chill. We have customers all day and we're open 24 hours and the night till only carries 50 dollars as a policy, although I've never had occasion to suspect we needed caution much. Past midnight, the only people passing through are truckers and skiers, and sometimes Benny the Indian comes in for a plug of Chattanooga Chew. Benny goes to the Mormon Church in town because they will pay his rent if he says he'll stop smoking. He hangs around the pop machine and fills a small Gulp with ice that he sucks on with his mouth open until we tell him to find some money or get out.

Put Crowsnest Pass anywhere urban, Vancouver or Toronto, or even Calgary for that matter, and what you have is a four-lane road, a freeway, but without the traffic. Here it's just a road for hikers or skiers or loggers to make their way up into the mountains. My station is past Frank Slide near Blairmore, just after the limestone boulders that cover the valley, at the mouth of the Pass. I work regular hours during the winter and then take off time during the summer to volunteer at the Frank Slide Interpretive Centre where I tell folks, kids, or senior citizens mostly, about when Turtle Mountain shed its limestone face and crushed the mining community of Frank below. In the winter, the center is closed and the boulders are covered with snow and the valley looks like a huge lumpy blanket. Only on the side of the road where the plow trucks spray salt as they pass can you see the boulders underneath.

Fender lives just up the road from the station in a hut not much larger than an outhouse. He's my assistant, has been for the past ten years. Every night I take all the cash and leave Fender with fifty bucks. During the night, he has customers, but they usually pay at the pump, swiping their cards fast as magicians. Fender has a Hells Angels tattoo on his arm though I've never seen him ride a bike. He takes his truck everywhere, a 70s-era Ford with monster wheels. I have him park the thing in back so there's room for customers. Fender's girlfriend is my cousin Annabel who works nights at the Day's Inn. She was a sprinter in high school and has calves the size of footballs. One summer she told me the only reason she's with Fender is because he's the only guy awake when she is.

The first time I caught a shoplifter, I called the cops and made the kid cry. He was a 14-year-old dropout who had to dump rock salt on the store's walk for community service. Now he's a cop, full-blown RCMP, but I still watch him whenever he comes in. Maurice is his name and he has a wife who works from home stuffing envelopes and a kid with an enlarged cranium and a woman who comes daily to help from social services.

Fender's an alcoholic and I've warned Annabel but she says that drink mellows him out. I tell her that his liver's going to rot, that he'll have to piss in a bag before he's fifty. My wife told me that every time I took a drink for the seven years we were married. After we divorced, I quit out of spite and now I can't stand the stuff. I enjoy a beer now and then, but gin, vodka, whisky, rum, the hard stuff I can't stomach anymore.

Maurice says he's had it with vandalism at the slide. People painting over rocks like they're subway walls. Benny says the slide has spirits that roam the rocks looking for their homes. I used to go cross-country skiing in the winter up at Allison Creek but I stopped on account of all the yuppies. Maurice runs the tracks on the weekends, carving grooves in the snow for the yuppie cross-country skiers from Lethbridge and Calgary and Fort Macleod. You don't think "yuppie" in southern Alberta, but every town's got them now.

On weekends I drive down to see my parents in Lethbridge at the new condos near the Lethbridge Lodge. The condos have a pool that's reserved for residents only. Since ninety percent of the condos are owned by octogenarians, most of the time the pool stays empty. Just a glassy surface. Put a few ferns and plastic roses around and people would think the pool was only for decoration. You go in the front door, and boom, there it is, a window looking out over the pool, with another window in the background so you can see the coulees.

Mom says I'm cynical because I won't live in the city. She has liver spots on her hands and last month she broke her collarbone from falling on ice. Her arm is in a sling, her hand limp as a dead fish, the spots front and center, impossible to miss. "Every time I change, it's a huge production," she says. Dad's La-Z-Boy has plastic cup holders in the arms. He grunts and changes to the weather channel where a hurricane blasts the coast of Florida.

One weekend Fender and Annabel invite me skidooing on my skidoos. We got almost 2 feet Thursday so we suit up and take my skidoos to Alison creek. Annabel is pissed about something and won't talk the whole way up and Fender makes it worse by commenting on everything he can think of about the weather and what he's going to do. "I'm going to get in some jumps," he says. "Snow is fucking sweet." I'm driving and have to pull over to put on chains before the switchbacks up to the trailhead. The trailer is heavy and my V6 Ranger can't take it. I tell Fender to give me a hand so he's not stuck with Annabel and her PMS.

"What did you do," I say.

"Come on," Fender says.

"You got issues? Did you knock her up?"

Fender kicks snow. "There's some things you shouldn't ask."

One time I covered for Fender on the night shift so he could take Annabel to Calgary for the weekend. He had won 500 bucks on Lotto 6/49 and was going to blow it all. Benny the Indian was there Saturday night telling me how to beat those machines in Walmart. He'd been to Lethbridge with his cousins, went to Iggy's until they got thrown out. There was a Checkstop on Mayor Magrath, so they took his cousin's truck to the Walmart and parked it there at three in the morning. At six in the morning, hung over and leaning on his cousin, Benny wakes up and there's a guy filling up the machines with stuffed animals. Benny can see him through the glass and the guy does a couple rounds on the machine and nabs one each time. Benny lost five bucks imitating the guy before he figured it out. "Got a whole closetful of Popples to prove it."

Mom can't get Dad to talk, calls me on the weekends to complain. "He just sits there watching the boob tube," she says. "And when I say something he snaps."

"Not your fault, Mom."

"Would you treat a normal person like that?"

My mother has asked me this before, several times. She repeats the question because she knows I don't listen either. It's during Stanley Cup playoffs, for Chrissake. I'm watching the tube too. "I don't know Mom."

"I think that he loves me, but he just doesn't like me."

Jagr is skating a good game, but Lemieux is in the box and the Leafs are on a power play.

"I said he doesn't like me."

Jagr battles along the boards with Sundin for the puck. He gets possession and ices it. The power play ends and the Penguins take a line change. I breathe out through my mouth. "Sure he does," I say.

My wife, before we divorced, wanted a child. She had charts of her cycle and would tell me all the signs of peak fertility: luteal phase, heightened temperature, cervical mucus. She used a thermometer daily, checked her signs, and wrote everything down in a scribbler that she wouldn't let me see. During the five peak days of fertility, we had regimented sex and she would speak to me in whispers, *come to me, fill me up, I want you hard.* She pulled and groped and lifted her hips up to mine and groaned and groaned when she came. Then she'd roll up in a naked ball, her hands around her legs and bum to the air so my semen worked its way in, my job as the sperm donor done.

During the summer once, Benny tells me about what really happened after the slide. The textbook story I've learned has the group holed up for fourteen hours before they dig their way to freedom. All seventeen survive. There are other miraculous stories: the Leitch family whose house is demolished and yet all three young daughters make it. The brakeman for the CPR who races across the rocks and stops an approaching passenger train. The Bansmer and Ennis families, miraculously surviving the destruction of their homes. There was another story about a horse that lived four days in the mine without food and water before people found him and let him out.

"They always tell the story of the survivors," Benny says. "They never tell about the ones who don't make it."

So he begins to tell me another story, not the one I'd memorized and carefully rehearsed. This one, all the Indians left the valley. There's a half-breed, a Métis who tries to tell the miners something's not right. The Indians believe shit like this. Like the rocks that used to dot the prairies, the Blood tribe's god Napi taking gobs of mud and breathing on them to make buffalo. Always an explanation. Benny tells me they knew a month in advance that the town would die.

"The miner told them to fuck off. The Métis guy, he told him the mountain would move. If he didn't get out of the way," Benny smacked his hands together, a horizontal clap. "Like a pancake. Guy didn't listen, never saw him again."

So they warned the town and the mountain moved. Now Benny says ghosts haunt the valley. They walk among the rocks but the landscape has changed and they don't recognize anything. "Imagine looking for home but there's no home to go to," he says.

The day we go skidooing, a big conversion van crowds the parking lot. You can see the lines crunched into the snow where their chains had been. I know we'll have to be careful that we don't plow anyone over, especially with the way Fender drives, taking jumps and whatnot. They are my skidoos after all. Annabel slams the door and heads to the port-a-potty, a green plastic box with about two feet of snow on top, piled high so you can see the layers like strata in rock.

Fender pops open a couple Exports and we clink them and drink to PMS. He downs his fast and meets Annabel halfway to the port-a-potty. They pass each other like two kids in junior high wanting to rough each other up.

"Guy's an asshole, what can I say," I say. The beer feels good, loosens me up.

"I should lock him in there," she says.

"Do, and I'm sure he'd dig out the bottom to get back to you."

"Didn't some prisoner escape that way?"

"Escape from shit-ca-traz."

Annabel does a drill sergeant about face and leaves me there holding my cold one. When she moves, she kind of sashays, a lot like my ex-wife. Everyone is reminding me of my ex-wife lately. The girl in the new GM commercial or Sandra from the bank. The GM girl has the same all-enamel smile and shoulder-length brown hair. She probably doesn't look anything like Jenny at all. The first time I took Jenny to see my parents, my mom took me aside and told me she was plain.

Once Benny came in with an open bottle of whisky and Maurice pulled up in his patrol car. Benny hung over the counter asking for $3 Scratch-and-Win Rummy. "I'm feeling lucky," he said. His hair was stringy, stuck to his face. His legs wobbled. Maurice turned on his lights and hitched up his pants before coming in. Benny didn't resist, just followed Maurice out and got in the back. Then Maurice came in for a pop, said, "I'll take him in until he dries out." Said it like he was real concerned. Maurice's lights blinked red and blue a couple times before he pulled out heading west into town. I bought the next Rummy ticket and won fifty bucks.

Mom tells me I need a hobby. "Skidooing's a hobby," I say.

"You need to meet a nice young woman."

"I'm not that young anymore."

Mom crochets while we talk. She's doing an afghan for her sister who is dead. Aunt May who died before her birthday, Mom's arbitrary deadline for the project. "Your father is not a nice man," she says. "But he's dependable. He's here. I don't have to worry about falling down and not having anyone there to help me up. You could have a heart attack, you know. Nobody would find you for weeks."

"Fender comes by," I say.

"A woman," she says.

"Only women are in bars," I say. "I hate bars." Which I do. Ever since I quit drinking the places drive me crazy. Benny sent the Mormon missionaries to my house once and we talked for an hour about drinking, the cycle of alcoholism. That's who will come by when I die. The Mormons will come and knock and see me lying on my floor, my face the color of chalk. They'll pound and pound and break the door down and baptize me now that I'm dead. Or have someone baptized for me–they explained it to me once. One of the missionaries was Elder Finch and he had a Bob Hope ski-jump nose and was from the UK. Blond hair the color of straw. He did the door approach: "We're from the chuhch of Jesus Chrahist, the Moohmons." An accent to beat all. Jenny would never let them in on account of a Mormon high school boyfriend who was always trying to get in her pants.

The day Jenny left me she said, "You are self-destructive."

When Jenny wanted children I was addicted to gambling. Would do anything to get in a game, drive to Fort Macleod or Lethbridge or Calgary if I had a mind to. Sometimes I'd leave for the whole weekend and come back piss poor. Or rich. Whichever it was, I would go back to try again, up the stakes, get in a better game. Texas Hold 'em, Omaha, 7 Card Stud, even Blackjack. I'd count cards, work out probabilities in my head. The probability that I'd be broke and sober by Monday morning.

"You don't act like you want children," Jenny said.

"But I do."

"Children are a big deal for me. It's my body that changes, my body that carries the child. I need the support."

"I support you."

"How?"

Benny doesn't come around anymore on account of Maurice who watches the place, drags him to the tank even if he's not drunk. He's home so infrequently now he says he's solved the problem of his rent.

On the skidoos I feel like Evel Knievel, like I've got lit gasoline in my veins. I love opening her up as I'm cresting a hill, the feeling when the carriage leaves the ground and my seat is up in the air. I fling my body into the turns so I can cut hard and snow flies in my face, misting my goggles in the moonlight. I'm following Fender as he zigzags through the woods around Allison Creek. Annabel is still pissed, won't even talk to Fender and drives straight like she's just waiting for us to get worn out and cut our engines, pack up, and go. At the ridge we wait for her to catch up and Fender says, "Why can't you just have a good time?" Annabel calls him a son of a bitch and guns her engine past him and down into the valley. From the ridge we can see the lights of Blairmore reflected against Crowsnest Mountain, a faint glow on the rock face. Snow clings to the rock like frosting. We're miles in now, high up, where the trees start to thin out and the trail widens, the snow deep and light. My skidoo hums in the deeper snow, the chain digging in, sending up a spray that fans out behind me like a tail, a goddamn snow white wedding train. Fender and Annabel are still sparring, weaving in each other's wake, cutting each other off. They're gunning for an accident the way they are driving, and it makes me cautious. Like I don't know a couple of drunks on snowmobiles in the backwoods of Crowsnest Pass aren't a recipe for disaster. I told Jenny once how much a kid costs from infancy to university before we jumped in the sack again to try and procreate. There is a wrong time for caution.

Another ridge, miles up now. Bowls of snow covering shale, the Rockies. Fender has his goggles on his forehead, is squinting down the trail into the beam of his headlight. Annabel crosses her arms above her head like she's doing the YMCA. Someone is out there, at the end of the cross-country ski tracks, skis knifed into the snow. I see them too: six solitary figures in a sort of semi-circle, waving, made more visible by the moonlight.

"Isn't it a little late for skiers?" Fender asks when I pull up.

"Late for anyone."

Fender gets another Ex from his pack, drinks it down and hands me the can.

"You've had enough," I say. Fender shrugs and Annabel says, "They're lost."

I turn around to look at her, moving my whole torso on account of my suit—a one piece with a hood that's like blinders for my peripheral vision. "We should help them," she says.

My father finally died of an aneurysm, quick and silent while he was watching reruns of *Hogan's Heroes*. Mom was in the back, in bed she claims. She had given up waiting for "the man" to come to bed, didn't see the point when she was tired and he had his shows. At the funeral, Dad wore the blue serge suit he bought for my wedding. A yellow tie with blue, pencil-width stripes. Mom insisted on saying a eulogy, even when there was a preacher and my Uncle Joe there to tell the story of his life: how he was the son of Ukrainian homesteaders who settled land near Bow Island. He was alive when the winter of 1906-1907 wiped out half of all the cattle in Alberta. Dad farmed his way into a business, sold his acres to the Hutterites, then started in on the grocery business in Lethbridge with no experience whatsoever. Uncle Joe told the story of Dad's life with selective memory, mentioning the grocery bit like it was pure entrepreneurial gold, like Dad hadn't sold the farm to cover his debts and bought into the grocery business just when chains like Safeway were closing them down. He didn't mention years of insurance sales or vans filled with vacuum cleaners that he'd peddle to retirees. At the end of the speech Mom held me by the arm and put a Kleenex to her nose, Dad's coffin still open from the head up, his face colored with foundation and blush that gave him the florid cheeks of a drunk or a blowhard, a preacher with fire in his lungs ready to raise Hell.

What I thought at the funeral was this: Dad was a man who always felt wronged. Like he'd done everything straight and the world never took notice. A dog who sits and rolls over and begs and plays dead and just waits on his haunches watching a fat man eat a pound of bacon.

A week after Dad's funeral, Maurice took Benny to a correctional facility. It was in the evening, in front of my store. Benny lay slouched up against a window, head lolling like a teenager falling asleep in class. I let him stay on account of the store being busy. It was a ski weekend. Folks were making their way back from Fernie, coming to fill up, their faces crisped by the sun, white where their goggles had been. A man with a Sun Ice jacket, arms marshmallow puffed, came to the register, said, "There's a drunk Indian on your doorstep." He leaned into me, almost whispered it, the strictest confidence. I nodded thanks, scanned his Snapple and rang up his gas. "Aren't you going to do anything?" He said. "Busy," I said. "Guy doesn't bother anyone."

Outside, I saw the Sun Ice guy on our payphone. Watched him step over Benny like he was avoiding a puddle. I waited for the guy to leave, then closed the till even though there were three people in line, tried to rouse Benny and get him to his feet. "What's the deal mister?" A man's voice behind me as the door swung shut.

"Benny," I said. "You have to get up, Benny."

"No place to go," Benny said. His hair was stuck to his face again, the rest of it matted around his shoulders. He smiled and shrugged, held up his hands like there had been something in them, lost now. "I can walk," he said, gently pushing me away. He stumbled off the sidewalk, pointed north, steady enough. I ran back in the store, resumed my place behind the register, hoping these well-to-do types weren't the kind to be fisting candy bars and pops while my back was turned. The customers kept coming: a 30-something frizzed blond with braces; two teenage boys still clomping in ski boots, toques a mile long down their backs; a family with two girls holding up giant Tootsie rolls like offerings, their dad paying cash, all business. I scanned and made change and rolled out pens and ripped receipts and popped the register, money filling up my coffers when I saw Maurice's blue-and-red lights through the window. Benny had come back, still drunk; he held a gas nozzle in his hand and kept trying to push past Maurice to fill a white Chevette that had pulled up. Maurice grabbed him by the elbow and Benny shook him off. Folks near the register followed my gaze; people in the store crowded the windows. A young man, teenager maybe, held up his hand to the officer. Benny turned his nozzle on the guy, then swung left and doused Maurice. He reached inside his padded jean jacket and pulled out a lighter, tried to light it but couldn't find a spark. "Holy shit," a guy in line said. Maurice sprang into action, bear-hugged Benny from behind, wrested the lighter from him and worked him to his knees.

We never saw Benny after that.

We get down to the clearing, the moon up full strength now, reflecting off the snow. A gibbous moon. "It's a gibbous moon tonight," I told Jenny once. "Waxing or waning?" she asked. A test I'd never passed. The boys are on their feet, their skis jackknifed, the snow stamped all to hell. A man with a grey beard, Wilbur-and-Ellis hat, and black fuzzy earmuffs smiles so wide he's liable to knock his muffs off. Fender cuts his engine, says, "You guys lost?"

"Scouts are never lost," Grey beard says, still smiling. "We just can't seem to find our way back to the trail head."

"Scouts, eh?" Fender turns his full torso to me, shrugs like what do we do next? The scouts shuffle forward in the snow; they're kids, mostly—maybe one other leader. No neat semi-circle now. I'm curious, so I ask, "What were you guys doing?"

Grey Beard steps up to me. Closer I see that the white in his beard isn't all hair but some is frozen lines of perspiration. He stops smiling and it looks like it takes a while for the muscles to relax. "We've been trying to get back for an hour now. Keep coming back to this spot. To tell you the truth we were praying."

"Praying!" Fender laughs. "I bet we're the goddamn answer to your prayers."

"Fender," Annabel says.

Fender says, "Lost and now you're found."

"You could say that," Grey Beard says.

Three weeks ago I saw Jenny in that mall in Lethbridge, the new one that's not so new anymore. I never go to malls. It was one of those things: a present for my mother, for her birthday; the mall was the closest commercial center to her place and I was late. I was in house wares, at the Bay. Young couples picked out wedding gifts for their registry; well-to-do women matched table settings with silverware. I was following a woman in her 70s who wore a pill box hat and white kid gloves, a teal two-piece suit made out of polyester, the miracle fabric. What kind of gift do you get for a woman pushing ninety who has just lost her husband? The woman with the pill box hat would lead the way. When I was young, Dad would get Mom power tools as a joke. Carbide drill bits, a Milwaukee Sawzall, fine chisels for duck decoys. What was the joke? He always acted like the gifts were for her. But now, shopping for my mother, trying to find something she would like, reminded me she was old too. Could die just as well. So I followed the woman, hands in my pockets, like I was an undercover security guard watching for the old lady to lift a paring knife and slide it into her sequined purse.

The woman surprised me by asking an employee, a kid with dyed hair and a piercing through his lip, about a cappuccino machine. Large cylindrical thing with levers and buttons, the kind you'd see in one of those new-age coffee shops without a customer over forty. That's when I saw Jenny, holding up her hand behind a plate of bone china, looking into the light. There was a salesperson, a woman with cropped hair so tight it looked like a wig. And there was a man, Jenny's man, wearing a cashmere coat, fingering the button just above his gut. Yuppies. Jenny picked up another plate and looked at it the same way, hand behind with the light streaming through it, the outline of her fingers faintly apparent. Then she turned in the light, to give the plate to her man and I saw it, the gentle curve of her abdomen beneath a smart knit blouse: the promise of a baby.

I'm thinking of this as a scout wraps his arms around my midsection and I signal for Fender to take the lead. Jenny and her pregnant body. We're out to save the scouts, get them back to hot cocoa and mothers and pajamas and the glowing embers of a fire. Annabel is beside me, parallel, saying "watch where you put your hands" but smiling, still a little drunk. The kid behind her doesn't know what to do, tries to hold onto the seat and almost knocks him and his buddy off when Annabel guns it up the hill. Then he's grabbing, reaching for anything to hold him through the ride. Me and my scouts start slower, pulling a pile of skis lashed to the emergency sled. The skidoo's engine is a dull hum getting louder, ready to shift gears. I can feel the scout's arms shaking as we speed up, creating our own wind chill. He is cold and happy, his prayers answered by a couple of drunks on skidoos and I'm thinking of Jenny and the fetus, of holding a light to her belly and looking for the faint outlines of a child. I'm thinking about fine bone china and stainless steel cappuccino makers and Benny dousing Maurice with gasoline, then lighting him on fire; I'm thinking of the pair of kid gloves I got my mother, like the woman in the pill hat, and the smell of limestone at the interpretive center, Maurice fisting candy bars and Turtle mountain moving, the blanket of stones and the obliteration of a town and the spirits that rise from the rubble, looking for home.

THE BEET FARMER

In town, Brandon shopped with his mother at a store
that sold name-brand clothing that other stores like the
Bay or Woodward's couldn't sell. The children's section
was filled with clothes on flat square tables. The clothes
had once been in neatly folded piles, the colors distinct
and separate, but now they were mixed together,
mounded like pitched hay bales. Brandon's mother pulled
out two new shirts. One was tan with a terry polo collar,
and the other was a brown heat-sensitive shirt that turned
red when you touched it. Brandon tried on the shirts and
Mom ushered him up past the cash register. Brandon
watched the clerk punch in the numbers. She was a girl—
twenty or so—with glittery-shadowed eyes. The numbers
were high and Brandon told his mother that they only
had ten dollars left from Dad's food allowance. She said,
"Does this look like food?" In the car he wriggled into the
heat-sensitive shirt and did up his seatbelt, turning the
brown hem red with his warm hands.

On the way home, they stopped at the sugar beet factory to take lunch to Dad. Mom handed him a blue tin
box splotched with paint like lichen. The factory was in
the middle of campaign, the busiest time of the year. The
day before, Dad didn't get home until almost 10:00 at
night, and work was at 6:00 the next morning. Campaign
had him going for weeks like that, until finally the beets

had produced all the sugar they would for that year. Mom told Brandon to lie low and make his way up to the main office that overlooked the rest of the factory. If Dad wasn't there, he could just leave it, then hurry back down to the Fairmont.

The factory smelled like molasses and swine. Brandon knew the smell from his Dad's Alberta Wheat Pool overalls, the ones that Dad rumpled in a metal bucket in the mudroom, where after work he would scrape all the organic sludge off his boots with a putty knife.

"You lost, son?" It wasn't his father, but a man with a straight-brimmed Wilbur-and-Ellis hat over a white hairnet and glasses.

"My dad works here," Brandon said.

"You're Tucker's kid. Up the stairs—you'll find him."

Brandon used one arm to lift himself up the stairs two at a time, with the lunch box swinging in his left hand, the way that the twelve-year-old deacons in his church carried the sacrament trays.

He didn't knock when he reached the door. Dad was there fumbling through the contents of a manila folder. His father still had on his overalls, with the dark stains like ink blots patched around his legs and midsection. Brandon handed him the lunch box.

"You got time to see the campaign?"

"Mom's in the car," Brandon said. Dad put the papers back in the folder, gave his son a hairnet and a hard hat, and pulled him downstairs onto the production floor. They walked around cylindrical vats, around pipes and steam and then out one of the doors. At the end of the yard, dump trucks rumbled their way up to a two-armed piler dumping beets in a pyramid-like pile. A couple of men operated the piler and three others stood with wide-mouthed shovels to catch any stray beets that may have missed the hopper. Four or five men, many also in overalls, stood with wide-mouthed shovels. The last truck pulled away prematurely, leaving a swath of beets near the hopper.

An older man with a pear-shaped scar on his cheek swore, clambered down from the piler, hitting a knobbed red kill switch on his way. The men gathered around the small beet pile with their shovels. "It's Tucker Junior," the older man said as Brandon and his father approached. The man wore a heavy cotton shirt with suspenders and his Wranglers had lines in the denim where his gut forced the material into rolls. Dad said that he was going to teach Brandon the trade, teach him how to be a real sugar beet farmer, and the men laughed. "I'm going to work here when I grow up," Brandon said. The man with the scar nodded approvingly. "Why not work here now?" he said.

"That's OK, Mitch," Dad said.

"Here's a shovel," Mitch said. He pointed to the pile of beets strewn near the mouth of the hopper. "Get that cleaned up and you can go home."

Dad turned to talk with the men and Brandon could hear them laughing. Brandon knew how to use a shovel. He went over to the pile and shoveled beets into the still hopper.

"Careful over there," Dad said.

Some of the men laughed. One said, "The boy knows his place."

Brandon was sweating and his shirt turned red with the heat. The shovel was almost as tall as he was with a metal blade and a wood shaft. The blade was horseshoe-shaped and about a foot wide. The loads got smaller until he could only manage to get a few beets into the hopper. But he kept going.

The men gathered and watched, talking back and forth to each other and remarking on Brandon's form. Brandon put the shovel with the flat back of it on the hard ground and scraped into the bottom of the pile. He scooped up about four of the muddy sugar beets like shrunken heads and heaved them into the hopper. He was tired and finally dropped the shovel. The man with the scar picked it up slowly.

"Like this," he said. He pushed Brandon back behind Dad, then walked over to the piler and pressed a large green button and held it down for a couple of seconds. The piler whirred to life, taking the beets up and over the arms where they piled on top of the pyramid. "Use your legs." He held the shovel across his torso, so that the wooden shaft rested on his gut. Then he bent his legs and shoveled the pile into the hopper in loads ten times the size of what Brandon had managed. The beets funneled out the bottom and onto the piler's conveyor belt. It was a solid stream of beets, moving up and out onto the pyramid, a long ribbon of brown.

The man with the scar turned off the piler, the last beets rolling down the pile.

"You really want to work, you can clean out that hopper," he said. "Skinny guy like you should have no problem."

He waited for Brandon to clamber down the muddy side of the hopper then he handed Brandon back the shovel. This time, Brandon held it like a pick axe and he whacked it against the mud-caked walls. Dirt and beets slid down out the bottom onto the still conveyor belt. The men, including his father, egged him on. "You'll make a beet farmer yet," they said. Brandon felt exhilaration, and although his choppy stabs didn't dislodge all the mud and debris, he felt that finally he was doing real, gut-wrenching work, the kind that he imagined his father did every day.

"Brandon!" It was Brandon's mother. He could hear her voice but couldn't see her until she was almost to the edge. The man with the scar helped him up in an arm wrestler's grip. The other men dispersed into the yard, pretending they were working, concentrating on their tasks like blinkered horses. "You didn't have to keep him," his mother said to Dad. "Now his shirt is all dirty."

"We were just having fun. Leave it alone," his father said.

"That's his good shirt," she said. "I just bought it. Can't you see?" She pointed at Brandon's chest where mud and beet juice stuck to his shirt. "We don't have the money."

Dad told Mom that he was just doing his job—if his money wasn't good enough, she knew what she could do. Brandon tried not to look at either of them, but instead played with the bottom of his shirt. One spot of red for each finger imprint, like daubs of fresh paint.

When Brandon's mother came back in the car, she closed her door, hard. She waited a moment and held her head forward, with the chestnut curls of her bangs reaching down to the steering wheel. She turned her head toward Brandon. In the light, he could see the small crow's feet around her eyes. She reached up to twelve o'clock on the wheel and started the car. The fan pushed lukewarm air through the vents, the air cold against Brandon's chest, browning his shirt so that the mud was less noticeable.

She turned the car's nose to the road. "You smell just like your father," she said.

WRITING ON STONE

It all started from a letter, a newspaper clipping of a tiny Cessna, crashed on the edge of a line of hoodoos. In the photo, a Mountie stood to the right of the wreckage, leaning over it with his hands at his sides, reverently, like he was bowing to a dojo. Four days previous, the ten o'clock news showed the same scene, only with blue smoke leaking out of the wreckage and into the sky where it fanned out against the push of a Chinook wind. It was March and there was no snow in southern Alberta.

If I had been one of the reporters on the scene, I would have covered the story out of guilt, for sending my cousin Mary the application for flight school. Mary was the pilot who flew the Cessna into the sandstone wall, a cousin whom I was in love with as a child. I had been a journalist in Toronto for the past fifteen years, long enough to lose contact with Mary, long enough to forget whether to turn before or after the plaster Allosaurus in Milk River to get to the hoodoos at Writing on Stone Provincial Park. And even though I sent a card, a letter, I still couldn't figure out why my uncle Elias Hofen, a Hutterite farmer who opposed me as much as he did Mary leaving, mailed *me* this article, an original, clipped out of Sunday's *Lethbridge Herald*.

So that night, I called my sister. Four rings and then a beep. *You've reached the Henleys.* Lana shut off the machine and I heard a familiar hello–different from the recording. "Elias Hofen-vetter sent me an article about Mary," I said. I wedged the cordless between my shoulder and ear, then pulled the string for the collapsible stairs and climbed up to the attic.

Lana was alarmed at the news. Not the accident–that she had heard–but at my uncle's apparent gesture of good faith, the address scrawled in his own hand: Wolf Creek Hutterite Colony. Newspaper without a note.

"He knows you liked her," she said. "It's not you he hates, it's Mom."

"You don't know that," I said.

My mother's family was still mysterious to Lana and me. Their beards, dark clothes, their unwritten Tyrolese German dialect. Every other Saturday, they drove into town in truckfuls, Luddite passengers using machinery for the good of the colony. Mom sometimes pointed them out, saying, "There's your Elias Hofen-vetter," or "There's your Martha-pasel." A wink or a nod was the only recognition of our family of four–the awkward family who bought their clothes, watched TV, and listened to music.

Mary was the only one I knew.

In high school I snuck into the Wolf Creek colony at night. Past the coulees near Ridge reservoir, the lines of silver grain bins. Later, when she was twenty-five and could choose to leave, I sent her an application for flight school. That was four years ago. Now, to Hofen, Mary was the casualty of a family of outsiders.

Lana said, "Remember when she followed your Houdini act? All tied up with her fists rubbed raw?"

"I do," I said, though it wasn't my act that stood out. It was right before Christmas at the only family reunion that I could remember. The colony had a history of celebrating Christmas with a Nicklus, a character somewhat like our Santa, but much more grotesque. Where Jolly St. Nick gushed a sort of overflowing charity and wellbeing, the Hutterite Nicklus was a fearful figure: stooped, grimy, with a charcoal face and a rope wig for hair. My parents hadn't prepared us for him. He lumbered into the room while we were talking and growled at the children in dialect. To us, he sounded angry and we crowded against my parents, listening for their translation: "He says that if you aren't good, you're not going to get any presents this year." The Nicklus put his arms above his head and roared at a small group of kids who screamed, then laughed. The parents shushed them and the Nicklus left a trail of presents that each child scooped up and opened eagerly. My parents then gave us each a gift. I received a set of magic ropes like ones that I had learned how to use from a friend. I started to show my cousins how they worked after everyone had recovered from the dreaded Nicklus and performed a series of escapes, sliding myself through the rope until I was free. Then Mary wanted to try. I showed her how to make the rope work, but she got the knots wrong and fell onto the floor. The colonists thought it was hilarious. But Hofen was angry, considered my performance worldly and vain, drawing too much attention to individual talents and abilities. He ordered the colonists to stop laughing, chided them for getting too riled up. Then he took my mother aside and we left, abruptly.

"I saw the accident on the news." Lana said. "It was lumped into a ten second aerial shot. Seems like the conservationists were more concerned about the damage it did to the park."

"It's things like this that make me think that God is a crook."

"A crook? I always thought of him as a slick used car dealer. Or a manly looking nun."

I tried to imagine Heaven, Mary walking up to the pearly gates and God slipping her into a used white Lexus. Leather upholstery. God dressed like a nun.

"Our virgin Mary," I said.

"Don't kid yourself," she said.

I like to avoid death. Real death, the deaths of people I know. Death in packages I can handle: humor, like the Darwin awards or the guy James Bond sticks with a spear gun, saying "I think he got the point." As a rule, I don't attend funerals. Memory is the reason. I had a recurring nightmare when I was seven years old where I imagined that I was stuck to the ceiling staring down at myself sleeping. From my perch I watched the covers rise and fall, then stop. The feeling afterward, waiting for what I comprehended later to be my own death, wasn't fear or anxiety, but guilt. It was wrong to be there, up on the ceiling, while the rest of me shuddered and died.

So when I bought the ticket to Calgary, my mom couldn't believe it.

I told her, I thought it might cheer people up.

My mother was there to pick me up at the airport, and on the way down to Ridgeview, she said, "Mary was a good pilot."

She said this to me like Mary hadn't crashed. Hands at ten o'clock and two.

I said, "She barely had her license. She was just learning."

"I don't think it's so simple," she said.

"What do the police say?"

"They looked at the black box, reviewed the 'evidence.' Sounded like a quickie to me. And the media's been having a heyday. The Writing on Stone 'Tragedy,' they call it. My word."

"I thought that you'd be more moved."

"Mary? I am moved. Moved and mad. I can just hear the Elders now, reciting the whole experience like it was a signpost for disaster. No one should ever have to leave that kind of a legacy. Dead for the communal cause. It makes me sick."

We passed Nanton, the spring water capital of Alberta. The plant had shut down because of cheaper competitors. I imagined all the water, pooling in rock cavities, erosion, wind, the sound of the water running through sandstone. I wanted to see the hoodoos. I told my mother this.

"I want to see the hoodoos."

"You what?"

"Where Mary died. The spot."

"It's your life," she said.

My mother has rejected much of what the colonists taught her, except her enduring work ethic and certain family traditions. My parents moved out of Wolf Creek colony before I was born. They were young, baptized members of the community and their departure meant excommunication. Even after my father died, she wouldn't talk about it, but I knew what it had meant for my father. He took an interest in taxidermy as a youth, starting with his moonlighting during the winter to make some extra pocket change trapping animals for their pelts. Early on, he learned the chemicals for tanning leather, for preserving the supple feel of the skin. He bought books on taxidermy and hid them in a chest in his attic. He became skilled at his trade and word got around. People from the community began coming to him, offering to pay handsomely for his trophies. My mother still had several of his creations: pheasants taking flight, foxes bent in a crouch. He had an eye for detail and his moulds were accurate and full. He truly enjoyed what he did. But the colony preacher usually dictated what Hutterite colonists could and couldn't do. Taxidermy signaled private enterprise and individualism, though at heart, I believe, my father was simply an artist, cobbling away with his tools, trying to create a living thing out of clay, glass, and flesh. As my mother explained it to me, my father didn't care about making profits or advertising. He simply worked to support his hobby and was honestly shocked when the colony preacher ordered him to stop. When my father wouldn't, Elias Hofen-vetter confiscated his taxidermy equipment, any trophies he had in progress, then put them in the central square where he burned them in front of everyone.

A year later my parents moved from the colony, though my mother said that her husband, as she knew him, was gone.

The next day, we drove to where Mary died. Writing on Stone started as I remembered it, a small mound growing to a mountain by the time we reached Milk River. At my request, Mom showed me the crash site, where for a moment the globular world of the hoodoos and Mary's Cessna blended together. It was before the Allosaurus statue that we turned, heading east, then wound down the road to the park.

Mary's crash site was over to the side, before the first of the larger hoodoos rose cliff-like against an oxbow in the river.

"There," Mom said.

There was a slope in the sandstone, then a dark gouge. The gouge was lighter at one end; it was coffee-colored, laced among the rocks like a stain. The wreckage had been removed—but by whom? And how did the Cessna get there, fallen out of the sky?

Mom said, "They say the altimeter or whatever you call it went haywire. Flew right into the ground. She was going to fly up north around Bear Lake Copper Mine, maybe do something with an oil company. That'd be a lonely life. Could you imagine, way up there? She must've been running away from something that caught up to her."

I knew what my mother wasn't saying. Suicide. Which wasn't fair, I thought, not for Mary. Or was it? I squatted, rubbed my hand across the sandstone. Tan, then black like a tire.

The government calls the park Writing on Stone because of the murals of buffalo hunts painted on the cave walls deep inside the hoodoos. The hoodoos themselves are just adornment—spires and grottoes of sandstone created by erosion. After seeing the crash site, we went to the murals.

Took the guided tour, the whole bit. I was hungry, and it was unseasonably hot. But I had never been before, my umpteenth time to Writing on Stone. It was my mom who finally convinced me to go. "I know how much you like coming home," she said. Mom called it home, though I felt more like a tourist in southern Alberta than anywhere.

During the tour, the guide pointed to a pair of eyeglasses carved into the stone and told us that they were two Native American warriors fighting. "Each circle represents a warrior behind a shield" he said. I took his word for it. There were four people on our tour: my mother and me, and a younger couple who appeared to be in love. The guy had on a pair of Wranglers and he wore a sweatshirt with "LCI" emblazoned on the front in green-and-yellow letters. The girl was much shorter. She reached up, put her head in the space between his shoulder and collarbone, pocketed her hand in the back of his jeans. She wore her hair pinned to the sides of her head, and when she turned to him, looking up from the spot nestled near his shoulder, her face looked like a half moon.

We reached a large room with three lines on top of an etched horse the size of a child. The tour guide pointed to the buffalo and fished for explanations. The couple, uninterested, moved next to the wall. I heard the rustle of clothes.

In high school, late at night, Mary and I used to exchange fantasies. Hers were predictable: there was always a man, a room, flowers, and a featherbed, but no sex, just kisses. I would start my fantasies with elaborate settings: private beaches, penthouses, Roman baths. I described the scent of the place, the steam from the baths, the wildflowers, ambrosia. I'd have the couple undress, not touching, then gradually embrace. Mary and I held hands. Then I'd have the woman reach for his penis and Mary would hit me on the shoulder. We could toy with each other this way for hours. There was a Quonset that the colonists used to store wood where we knew no one would interrupt us. We'd glide through in the dark until we found a dry spot to lie on our backs.

"Come on," I told her once, "you don't even have to feel your way."

"Let's stop here," she said. I remember that at the side of the Quonset was a sliding window that was open. Just one spot where threads from an outside lamp streamed through. Mary held out a hand. In the light, it looked like her fingers were orphaned from the rest of her body. I reached for her fingers instinctively, to hold them before the moment was gone, washed out by the autumn night.

"Tell me another fantasy," she said. It was safe—two cousins—no fear of relationships, commitment, duress.

We groped for each other in the dark.

The tour guide asked another question, demanding that everyone, all four of us participate, raise our hands if we knew the number of national parks in Alberta, and who could tell him what they thought the curving lines from the neck of the engraved warrior represented? The girl in love answered with a question: "A headdress?"

"Right," the tour guide said. Then the guide explained how the native Blackfoot used to hunt, why they recorded their exploits in these caverns. The Blackfoot used animal oils and grease for paint, giving their figures life.

Back in Ridgeview, my mother told me that whenever I visit, I spend all my time hiding. "You don't phone any-one," she said. "People have a right." Truth is, news catches up with me. In rural Alberta, I always feel pursued. It's not like Toronto. People know me there, sure, but here it's everybody. Doug Coppins still mans the post office, drag-ging his palsied foot to the mailboxes. Stuart Halpern is at Fraser Foods. The high school kids drive their trucks up and down the street, stopping to talk, reaching out to each other like they're at a tollbooth with time on their hands.

In Ridgeview, the streets are as wide as a three-lane highway. People park in the middle. Every dog on the west side of town is related.

My mother's comment bothered me, so I called Lana again. I told her about Writing on Stone and that Mom thought I was in hiding.

She said, "Have you been to see Elias Hofen-vetter yet?"

"How do you stop in and see someone you've never really talked to?"

"You don't. You phone and ask first. And be polite."

"That's a thought," I said.

"Do Hutterites have phones?"

"Sure they do," I said. "They're not Amish."

"There you go. Look in the phone book."

Downstairs, my mother turned on the stereo. Classic rock, Righteous Brothers. Her music.

Lana said, "Maybe you could try stopping by when it's convenient, with an introduction. Go on Sunday, after supper. How long are you staying?"

"Until Monday."

"He did send you the note. Take it as an invitation."

The Righteous Brothers sang, "You're my soul and my heart's inspiration." High and in harmony.

"And what should I say?"

The music was loud when I reached the landing, phone in hand. My mother looked small. She had refinished the kitchen and it seemed immense around her, her dark hair pulled up in a bun and her forearms bare on the counters. She snapped beans on the counter and moved to make space, pushed a yellow bowl towards me.

I walked close to the sink with my hands clasped behind my back. It seemed ridiculous that my mother should still be there when her kids were elsewhere. Me in Toronto, Lana in B.C. Nothing in the area except bad memories, scars in the earth, disgrace.

"Lana thinks I should stop by the colony."

"Do you have an invitation?"

"Uncle Hofen's clipping is as good as any."

"That's what you think," she said, shaking her hands into the sink. She reached in the cupboard for a pot, placed it under the running water. "They want you to think you're welcome. For all you know he sent it to you to show you what you did to his daughter."

"You can't always expect the worst."

She put the beans in the water, brought them over to the stove to boil.

"It's too bad Mary died, but you can't go thinking that will make Hofen or anyone out at Wolf Creek come associating with us Gentiles for the long haul. Even if they are family. You're cut off and that's it."

I took a walk down Main Street the next day. It was cold, so I stopped at Fraser Foods to warm up. It hadn't changed its sign in fifteen years, white with blue curlicue lettering. Home Hardware was next door, though I always thought of them as one store because the aisles were connected in back. You could walk a beeline from the frozen meats straight to a row of air compressor accessories, hoses, and pneumatic attachments. I took my time down the aisles, rubbing my hands together for warmth. Then the front door opened and several Hutterite women came in. I forgot that it was Saturday, the day they stocked up on canned goods that they couldn't get elsewhere, sometimes buying extracts or ingredients for the lavish communal meals they made where they fed the men first, then ate with the children at a separate table. The women's kerchiefed heads disappeared around a corner. I watched the polka dots and the colorful fabric of their dresses. I didn't know if they were from Wolf Creek, but I thought that I'd check the hardware department anyway, looking for the men's black felt hats. I passed rows of pliers, screwdrivers, and gardening supplies before I saw three Hutterite men lined up at different places along a row of plumbing parts.

One of them held up a copper elbow joint and fasteners, showing them to a shorter man with glasses. The third man was the farthest from me, but I recognized him by his height–Elias Hofen-vetter. I hugged the end of the aisle and picked out two different paint rollers wrapped in cellophane. I couldn't decide whether or not to approach the group. You see, I wanted to talk to Hofen. But I was curiously afraid. Instead, I waited and bent down on the ground so that I had access to a bin of brushes. The tag said that they were on sale, so I took a couple and I kept watching Hofen until he left the rest of the group, walked over an aisle and started going through a pile of metal boxes. I pretended to be searching through some light switches and outlets, all marked down to 49 cents. I picked out a couple and moved closer. His beard was the same as the pictures I've seen, the same as I remembered him as a child. There were only a few brief memories I had like this, shades of my uncle now rifling through pieces of metal. I was grateful and confused by the encounter. Under scrutiny he bore almost no resemblance to Mary. He had a foreboding profile: chin hidden under a beard, his head bound by the black felt hat. Only his nose resembled Mary's, with its round tip and nostrils. On his head, it appeared small, dwarfed by his other features. But I was positive that it was Mary's nose, a living reminder of the daughter he'd buried a week before.

I counted out five smaller electrical boxes, then moved back down the aisle to get covers for the outlets and switches. Authenticity. Three switches, two outlets, covers for each, and five boxes. By this time, my Uncle had moved back down the aisle, so I gathered everything together and stood behind him in line. Still no recognition. I could smell his coat, a mix of barley feed and engine oil. His hands were shaped like wrenches. I watched him go through the line, pay cash for his products. He put the receipt in a bag, then waited and turned around, stopping to talk in line with the Hutterite behind me. The cashier ran up my total and I got out my checkbook. "No personal checks," the cashier said. It was a girl, perhaps a Waldner. I couldn't place her.

"I think my mother has an account," I said.

"What's her name?"

My finger held a check over the plastic flap. I unclicked my pen and the cashier finished bagging my outlets. I put the checkbook in my pocket, then made the mistake of looking left, behind me, to Hofen and the other Hutterite standing in line. Her name? I thought. What is her name? I gave the answer over the counter, grabbed the bag, and fled.

At home, my mother looked through the bag. Saw the outlet covers, the switches.

"Some things I picked up at Home Hardware," I said.

She held up a pink roller. "You going to do some painting?"

"I didn't mean to buy them."

"You didn't mean to?"

I told her the story, Hofen standing at the checkout counter, jumping when he heard her name. I could see him through the window, his image blurred by the swinging door, the advertisements frosted into the glass. My mother laughed and laughed.

For a long time, I was in love with Mary. We were cousins, kissing cousins, and we went through great lengths to meet. We found ways for her to shirk domestic chores, to free up time to see each other on Saturdays when she came into town. One night, in the Quonset, we planned to go bridge jumping. The next day Mary was supposed to be gathering chokecherries and saskatoons with the other girls from the colony, but a friend said that she would cover for her. When you were in the brush, it was easy to get away. Berry picking could take hours.

"I don't have a suit," she said.

"I'll think of something."

I found an old swimsuit of my sister's, then a pair of
shorts and a t-shirt. I met Mary at one of the irrigation
canals a couple of kilometers down from the ridge spill-
way, not far from Wolf Creek. The bridge that crossed it
was used by service vehicles and it was only accessible by
an overgrown gravel road. Our old conversion van navi-
gated the potholes and brome grasses that claimed the
middle of the road, and I waited for Mary there, parked on
the bridge, watching the skyline for her approach. I should
have been able to see her for miles, her black dress con-
trasting with the prairie taupe. But she surprised me by
appearing from under the bridge, sliding the van door
open, and jumping inside.

"Turn on the air conditioning," she said. "It's so hot."

I got in the driver's seat and turned it on. Mary loved
the tiny deprivations of Wolf Creek and always made it a
point to let me know she was different from the more
orthodox Elders. She was always surprising me, producing
pirated cassette tapes of country singers and sometimes
cigarettes. At the time, I took her caprice and daring as
signs of good faith, of interest; the more I persisted in my
affections, the more she showed me what she knew about
the world. Now, I see that those same gestures may have
revealed an insecurity, a twinge of inferiority or shame.

"I got some things for you," I said. I hoped that the suit
fit, though I had the t-shirt and shorts just in case. I wanted
her to feel comfortable, to have fun.

"I'll need help out of my dress."

I hadn't thought of that. "OK," I said.

I turned on the radio. It was Garth Brooks. I helped her
undo the buttons on the back of her dress, and she slowly
unsheathed herself, like she was peeling off a layer of skin.
She wore a cream cotton slip and there was a distinct tan
line where the high cut of the dress met her neck.

"I'm glad that you brought the van," she said. "For
privacy."

I hadn't thought of that either. In fact, I had merely

thought of the van as a vehicle for jumping off. Without it, the water was only ten or twelve feet under the bridge; with the van you got a few more.

"I brought one of Lana's suits," I said.

"Thanks."

She turned towards me and reached for the suit. She brought it slowly to her chest and she smiled. I kissed her then. She dropped the suit and kissed me back, lying down next to me. We stopped kissing and she laughed, then guided my hands to her breasts. But when I reached for her hand and fumbled with the knot on my shorts, she withdrew. "This is enough," she said, taking my face in her hands.

Mary changed into her suit and put on the t-shirt. "So as not to attract attention," she said. I put some towels on the hot van roof, then we climbed on top and jumped off— first together, waving hands and screaming—then separately, me diving, Mary still jumping straight, moving her arms in circles as she sliced through the air and into the water. We jumped and dove until we were both worn out. Mary stretched out on the roof of the van and I leaned over the bridge railing, casually throwing stones into the water and looking for catfish. Then I noticed a Chevy barreling up the road, kicking up dust from the gravel that spread out behind it like the tail of a comet.

"Mary," I said.

She looked up and squeaked, then jumped right off the roof and into the water. She splashed around to the side and waited there. I leaned over and she waved at me. "Go, go," she said. "But throw me my clothes!" I found her dress, her practical shoes and underwear and threw them down to her. I watched long enough to see her black polka-dotted kerchief land in the water and see Mary wading out to it. I ducked into the van, started it up, and left in the direction opposite of the approaching truck. I knew most likely who it was behind me, but I left Mary there anyway, in my cowardice.

A week later, I received a letter in the mail from Elias

Hofen-vetter himself, forbidding me to come near the colony, much less see his daughter.

Saturday night, I searched downstairs for my old childhood trunk. It was in the cold storage room, next to a bag of wheat. I dragged it along the cement, lifted it over the doorjamb and took it into the family room. The box was disorganized but comprehensive, a collage of my life. I didn't know what I was looking for. I read old journals from grade 2, looked at class pictures and old report cards. There were Christmas ornaments made out of clay, a story I wrote about a werewolf, letters I received from old girlfriends. I read each piece of my history as though they were artifacts and I was trying to piece myself together. "Eric is an alert and sensitive child," one teacher wrote. Another said, "He draws inappropriate pictures." At one point, my mother came down and told me that she was going to sleep. I told her that I would see her tomorrow. I looked at my watch. It was past midnight. I took off my watch and threw it on the couch.

The pile enthralled me.

I found several high school mementos: pictures of graduation, a gold rope for academic excellence, petrified shells from a choir trip to Vancouver, and a box containing old toenails that fell off after a skiing accident. Then I found two scribblers full of poems that I wrote while I was in love with Mary. The cover was missing from one and the pages were curled and water damaged. I had kept the poems to myself, hid the notebooks so that no one would know that I had written them. Strange. The measures I took to ensure their secrecy eclipsed those that I had taken to keep in contact with Mary. I didn't know why. Perhaps it was because age had made me aware of the taboo of two cousins in love.

Underneath the poems were clothes and a mop with an attached comb headpiece. For a Nicklus, my Halloween character of choice for years. Simple, scary. Not sure it was a man or a woman, the eyes blacked out with charcoal. I put it on. The corded wig drooped down over my eyes. I reclined on the couch and fell asleep.

I woke up in the afternoon alone. There was a note on the couch that read "Out to help Gloria with her chickens." That was my mother. Even when people came to visit, she couldn't stop working. I got up and went into the bathroom. My eyes were red from sleeping in my contacts and my face was streaked with lines from where I had slept on the corded wig. Pathetic. I had less than a day left to see my uncle, and here I was, hiding. I resolved to go to Wolf Creek that night.

I went to the colony in my mother's Honda. I had been drinking. I was still in the cord wig but had added the getup that I found in my trunk downstairs and blackened my eyes with charcoal. I was a Nicklus, ready to hit the colony and raise hell. On the road, I didn't like how my mother's car was handling. Was it that I was drinking, plowing my way through the new gravel, artificially trying to drum up the courage to meet my uncle dead on? Or had I just been away for so long, that I had forgotten how to negotiate the shifting surface? Each corner I took almost sent me fishtailing, the new gravel spitting off to the side. I was over adjusting. I forgot that driving on gravel was like driving on ice. Just let the car go where it wants. Don't jerk the wheel, decelerate by downshifting, don't use the brake.

I saw Wolf Creek's lights near the bottom of a hill. There were more Quonsets, more outbuildings and residences, all with the same white clapboard siding, and all devoid of any exterior decor. Something about the place always made me feel guilty. I signified worldliness. Since moving to the city, I had an acute understanding of economics. In the colony, everything was literally black and white. The clothes they wore were black, the buildings white. The only color permitted was on the women's dresses, but never in the church

except for weddings. An outsider like myself was marked.
There were watches, jewelry, icons on your clothes, your
vehicle. Even driving in a car, to them, was worldly. It
wasn't a truck or a van, something that they could use for
the colony. Even the lower middle classes, which made up
most of Ridgeview, were marked by vanity.

I had written an article once in *The Globe and Mail*
entitled "The Paradise of the Prairies," describing the simple rural life and communal living of the Hutterites. In it, I
praised the Hutterites' division of labor, their industrious-
ness, their harmonious living. I summarized their history,
their migration to the US and the martyrdom of two conscientious objectors who were drafted into the US army
during WWI and beaten to death by their fellow soldiers–
an event that prompted the Hutterites' immigration into
Canada. I glossed over the usual contentions of their being
wealthy landowners who put rural farmers out of business.
I called the colonies "pearls of Canadian multicultural-
ism," a "vibrant patch in the fabric of Canadian identity."
I'm not sure why I chose such a rosy slant, but the feed-
back that I received was tremendous. "Excellent," my editor had told me, "just the kind of cross-cultural understanding we need." But now, sitting in my ditched car, idling
about fifty meters from Wolf Creek, I felt like a jackass.

You see, I was more than a little drunk. It was Sunday
night, almost midnight. Wolf Creek had long finished its
religious services and the children had said their prayers.
Hofen was probably curled up next to my Martha-pasel in
bed at the far end of the main longhouse. I was a Nicklus,
the fearful Christmas imp with a mop of corded hair and
charcoal for eyes, wearing a beggar's garb, my pants split
in the knees and seat, the heels of my boots worn down to
the wood. I left the car where it had fishtailed into the
ditch and walked the rest of the way to the Colony. There
was no gate, just a grid of gravel roads in between white
houses, lit up by occasional lights. When I passed the
Quonset near the entrance, exterior lights came on. I wan-

dered to the nearest longhouse, tried looking through the drawn shades. I knocked. The windows opened, a child peered out, screamed. More lights. I found an open door; no one locked them there, and I held the knob and waited for my dizziness to subside. A man came while I was pressed up against the pane and I turned my head, squishing my charcoal nose against the window. He was wearing his pajamas, a woolen one piece, and he pushed the door open. Was it my uncle? Elias Hofen-vetter? I felt the man's thick hands on my collar. *I'm Nicklus,* I thought. *Aren't you afraid?*

I wanted the man to be angry with me. To use the strap, like the German teacher. Ten whacks on my open palm. I wanted him to break tradition, get out the gun locked away in his attic, the one they used for gophers, and point it at me, force me staggering off their property.

More lights. People. A boy in a cap, girls in white night-gowns. Men shouldered their way through them, in front.

The man said something to them angrily in dialect. Then I heard a laugh. Another of the men responded. I pulled at the thick cords of my wig and it slid off my head. My head was slick with sweat, even in the winter cold. More laughter.

"A Nicklus, eh?" one of the men said to me. "Thought you'd scare us good?"

The man swung me onto his back like a sack of flour. I tried to tell him that I could walk. He shouldn't bother. I heard the low rumbling sounds of the men talking. The crowd dispersed. People helped me through a door, turned on lights in an austere room. No carpet. A cot. I was placed on the bed, my worn boots removed. Then I was turned on my side and tucked in, like a baby.

I woke up the next day horribly hung over. I had missed my flight. Someone had removed my clothing and placed me in one-piece pajamas. The room was spare, without any wall hangings. The floor was tile and the bed I was sitting on nestled comfortably in a corner. The bed had no end posts, no decoration carved into the wood. Flat, straight, simple, and sturdy. I got up and walked to a small table and two chairs at the end of the room that were next to a large window. Outside children played a game on stilts. A boy, on the brink of adolescence, controlled it. He had that pre-puberty command of his body and the stilts functioned like extensions of his legs. The other children, girls in their winter dresses and boys in black jackets, tried to keep on their stilts, but failed. The one boy was king.

The door opened. "Thought you'd like some coffee. Wake you up."

My uncle, Elias Hofen-vetter walked through the door balancing a tin tray carrying two glasses and a pot of coffee. I imagined it was rare for a Hutterite man to be serving, but I realized that I didn't really know. Was it normal for him to be there taking coffee with me rather than in the communal mess hall with the other men? I wanted to ask him.

"Thanks," I said.

Hofen drew the other chair away from the table and bent with difficulty to sit down. He seemed remarkably old. His beard was grey and white and the hair on his head was thinning. He wasn't wearing his hat. He crumpled his hands together in his lap, the fingers intertwined, caked with calluses.

"You gave us quite a scare last night," he said. He didn't say it accusingly, but I wondered at his sincerity. Too many years in journalism, trying to minimize biases with forced objective prose.

"I'm sorry," I said.

"Quick to profane, quick to apologize," Hofen said.

"I guess."

"Still a young *towga nixer.*" He laughed.

"A troublemaker?"

"That's right."

I'm not a coffee drinker and the coffee was lukewarm. I

took gulps, one by one. I was conscious of the sound each gulp made, the opening and closing of my epiglottis, the liquid sliding down. Hofen nodded as I drank.

"Eric," he said, "why are you here?"

I put the coffee mug on the table. "You sent me the article from *The Herald*. About Mary. I'm not sure that's why I came or not. But here I am." Outside the king-boy gathered up the stilts from each of the children. He and another boy carried them to a longhouse running parallel to the one we were in and stood them up in a diminishing drift of snow, held only by the shadows of the building that flanked it.

"They're going to ruin the wood," Hofen said. He shook his head.

"I'm sorry about Mary," I said.

Uncle Hofen suddenly stood up and walked to the window.

It was the boys. I could see them, too. They picked out icy chunks from the sliver of snow and flung them at a group of girls using slingshots made from old inner tubes and willow branches. Hofen abruptly opened the window and yelled across the field. They stopped immediately. The one who had been so proud on the stilts gathered up the four slingshots from each of the boys and gingerly walked to our window.

"That's Marcus," my uncle said. "The boys will follow him anywhere. Could lead them right off the colony if he wanted to." The boy brought over the slingshots and Hofen closed the window, shutting out the early spring chill.

"Must be hard," I said.

"Only when they don't come back. The boys, you know, they go into town and get a job. Get a few dollars to spend in the world. Then they notice that people think they talk funny. They try to meet English girls and find they have nothing to say. That's when they come home. Everyone welcomes them. Welcome even people like you."

He sat down and handed me one of the slingshots. They were finely made, sturdy and practical.

"What about Mary?" I asked. "Would you have welcomed her?"

Hofen smiled, a mixture of sadness and pity. "What do you think, young *towga nixer*? Of course I would have. She was my daughter."

My uncle reached out for the slingshot that I was fiddling with and I started to cry. No real reason for it except being hung over and wanting forgiveness. I had done wrong. I wanted to rewrite this story, change the way that I had come here out of the darkness. But time had taken that option away. I had my life. I thought how, in a few hours, I would be waiting standby in the pre-flight lounge at the Calgary airport, then flying east. There would be questions in the office: How was your weekend? Where did you go again? I'd catch up with the writers who covered for me and then I'd go to lunch with the Leisure editor to sample a new restaurant downtown. So different from me now, the Nicklus, crying over a wooden toy while my uncle watched me cautiously, wondering how the two of us came to be there at the same table, occupying the space with our sorrow.

DUMMY

IT'S NOT EASY, BEING GREEN.

–KERMIT THE FROG

I could feel Jordan's hands working up and down my back. He tweaked my shoulder blade and my left arm waved. He pressed his fingers against the base of my neck and my head flopped forward. I maintained the almost plastic smile that I needed to play my part. My limbs dangled like they were made of wood, waiting for his hands to move to where my muscles were twitching, ready.

"And now, I will drink this glass of water while my dummy, Eric, recites 'Hey Fiddle Diddle' in falsetto."

Jordan reached for a transparent tumbler and I tried to remember the words to the nursery rhyme. Every night it was a different line. Sometimes I sang the Canadian national anthem in a burly vibrato, or songs from *The Wizard of Oz* or *Charlie and the Chocolate Factory*, depending on the audience. He had pushed me out on a limb before. Once I had to make up the words to the U.S. Pledge of Allegiance to a truckload of high school baseball players from Montana. Most of them thought it was hilarious, but at the end of the show, a couple of the chaperones demanded their money back. And "Show Biz," even if it was just summer stock, took that seriously.

"You don't know the Pledge of Allegiance?" Jordan asked after our number.

"Nope," I said. And frankly I didn't care. One girl three rows from the front with red ringlets for hair laughed so hard that she had to lean forward in her seat. That was reward enough.

"Let's just hope they don't have guns."

His concern, like everything Jordan did, was an act. Our number opened the rest of the evening up to Canadian-American jokes that riffed through just about every sketch that followed. Sometimes you just had to find the pulse of a group, and that night thrumming our neighbors south of the border was it.

I started my recitation, and this time I acted like I was gurgling. I tried to sound like those cartoons in the '40s where the characters are underwater and the soundtrack warbles. I had done this before, several times. It all depended on what I thought the audience's expectation was and if my behavior would somehow thwart it. Sometimes the irony was too thick for some–too idea-oriented. A real person pretending to be a dummy, then screwing up the lines? Usually it worked. Funny.

Jordan stopped drinking and I changed my voice, finishing the nursery rhyme in falsetto: "And the dish ran away with the spoon." I turned my head like it was on a swivel, and looked at Jordan who frowned dramatically.

I got the job at the old Empress Theatre in Fort Macleod after singing "Ain't She Sweet" during an audition at the Yates. The year before, the Empress's Great West Summer Theatre troupe had an argument about the leasing terms and decided to go elsewhere. When their troupe dissolved, the Fort Macleod mayor opened up the summer months to bidding. The Star Singers of Lethbridge got the bid and held auditions at the Yates.

Jordan was there.

He made an impression. He had straight red bangs that hung down to his chin, and during the improv sketches, he walked with purpose, pushing back with his feet so that he looked like he was moving far and fast. He always cut across stage in diagonals, to show depth. And he never turned his head away from the audience. When he sang "Stars" from *Les Misérables*, several fellow auditioners clapped. *Les Mis* was still new then. I remember that he forced a vibrato.

Star Singers hired four guys and four girls to make up the cast. I was the youngest of the group, and shy. "Shocked" would be the best word to describe how I felt. I was from Ridgeview, a town that had fewer inhabitants than the other cast members' high schools had students. The rest of the cast had experience in drama clubs, show choirs, and improv. I sang and played the piano and violin, but I had very little acting experience—just a few parts with the Ridgeview Playhouse as a kid. I was surprised that they hired me.

My mother wasn't. "You should've seen yourself up there," she said after I finished singing my audition piece. "A regular little showman." We had practiced the song "Ain't She Sweet" with a few cheesy hand gestures and stage movements. When I sang, "Just cast your eye in her direction," I swept a hand cross-wise in front of me like I was measuring the horizon. I molded my hands in the form of a woman's curves. "Ain't that perfection," I sang.

I took the back staircase down to the dressing rooms. Sam was donning his maître d' shirt for the Roadkill Café sketch. I had five minutes to mess up my hair with gel and cover my face with bruise-like splotches of makeup. Sam was eighteen, only two years older than I was, but looked thirty. He started bartending illegally at the end of grade ten, before he was even sixteen. He had three goals in life: to be a bartender, to be a professional actor, and to make a million dollars. "Two out of three," he told me the first week that we worked together. He left and I turned to the mirror.

I've always prided myself on my face's elasticity. How I can mould it like Play-Doh to do whatever I want. There are twenty-four muscles in the human face, an infinite number of expressions. Jordan said that for hours, he would stare at his image, going through every nuance in expression, just so that he would know how his face worked. You had to be very particular, he said, to be an actor. That first week in May, Ben, Sam, and I were going through the Roadkill Café sketch, just brainstorming for ideas while we watched Jordan loudly talking to himself on an empty row near the Empress stage. Ben started laughing. "Do you need someone to talk to?" he yelled over. Jordan kept talking to the wall. "I don't think so," we could hear him saying. He shook his head. "Stupid, stupid, stupid." By the end of the summer, we'd all be doing the same thing, trying to get into character.

Backstage, in the dark, I could see Kelly changing into her "Black Velvet" Alannah Myles outfit. She attached inserts inside her cream-colored bra to make herself more chesty. She only had a few minutes before we'd be done with our scene and she didn't have time to trek down below the stage and into the hallway that cut through the bottom of the Empress. Every day I thought she was embarrassed as I watched her undress, although it never bothered her when Jordan was around. We often came into the girls' dressing room for makeup or props and all four of the girls would be in various stages of dress. When Jordan entered through the swinging door, they greeted him like one of their own. When I followed behind, Kelly reached for a towel to cover up.

"Waiter, there's a fly in my soup," Sam said.

"Oh, I'm so sorry. Igor!"

It was my cue. I staggered onstage, dragging a palsied right foot. I had cotton balls in my mouth and my face looked like it'd been run over by a semi. I dumped a bag of black plastic flies into Sam's bowl, waited for Ben's clap, and I lumbered back. Exit stage left.

The first few days of rehearsal, I wouldn't talk. I could imagine Jordan, Carli, and Bernice meeting together and discussing my reticence as they would a lack of funding or a freak accident. They would look for blame, try to figure out a way to circumvent it. "He seemed so outgoing," they'd say of my audition. "I had no idea."

Truth is, the cast intimidated me. There was Lynette Hamilton, the brunette who had tap danced at the Jubilee Auditorium in Calgary; Austin who had won international awards in the Lethbridge Jazz choir two years running; and, of course, Jordan, the creative genius who was finishing up his second year in acting at the University of British Columbia and had played any number of roles from Winthrop in *The Music Man* to the lead in *Sweeney Todd*. The cast were all ostensibly extroverts and when we first rehearsed they swarmed the stage with impersonations and improv. It was like being in a room with Tracy Ullman and Robin Williams competing for airtime and I was the straight man, the dummy who couldn't talk.

Some of the things they did embarrassed me, like when Jordan lined us up on all fours and checked if we were breathing from our diaphragms. He made us pant. "Good, good," he said, the harder we panted. He seized my midsection like he was squeezing a bellows.

"We're going to play *Freeze*," Bernice said. "Eric, you should like this."

I shrank into my seat.

"Carli and I will start acting out a scene. At any point, one of you can yell 'Freeze,' then take the sketch any direction you want."

They acted a birth. Carli, who used to dance professionally in Chicago, played an orderly who had to take care of Bernice until the doctor arrived. She pretended to hook up an I.V. and stick a needle in Bernice's rear. Everyone laughed like it was a regular party. Bernice, who had two boys of her own, puffed out her cheeks, held her abdomen, and hyperventilated. She leaned forward to take pressure off her back and Sam yelled "Freeze!"

He tapped Bernice on the shoulder, took the exact position that she was in, then pretended he was a golfer bending over on a putt. "Caddie," he said. "Pitching wedge."

He placed the pitching wedge on the ground, swung hard, and threw his club when he realized that he'd missed. The caddy knelt down to pick up the imaginary club that Sam had thrown, and Jordan yelled "Freeze!"

He took Carli's position with one knee on the ground, then raised his head and said, "Alice, dear Alice, I've been thinking about this a long time. Last night I withdrew all my government savings bonds and cashed in three hundred thousand aluminum cans to give you this." He held his hands forward and said, "Creak," as he opened the box. "It's an engagement ring."

Sam, as Alice, swooned, sat down on Jordan's knee and put his hand in his hair. "For me?" he asked.

"Alice, will you marry me?"

Sam took his hand from Jordan's hair and smiled, pretending to hold the ring in his hand. I yelled, "Freeze!"

Back in the dressing room, I noticed it. A note, under a daisy in a vase. Condensation had dampened a ring into the yellow Post-it. "Sam," it read. "I consider you my closest friend." Jordan's frenzied initials marked the bottom of the note. I had seen those same letters scrawled on so many programs when we stood in lines after every performance, thanking patrons on their way out. I often garnered attention from younger girls or older women, who thought my rendition of Kermit the Frog's "It's Not Easy Being Green" (replaced with the words, "It's Not Easy Being Dumb") hopelessly endearing. Jordan always attracted a different crowd–displaced urbanites or other actors, friends from Lethbridge or Vancouver. He scribbled his initials, "JP," then added quips from old song titles or the Muppets.

Now, looking at the Post-it, I felt the weight of my intrusion. I had shared a dressing room with Sam the whole season, spent nights at his house, gone with him to parties and publicity events. And this square piece of paper somehow claimed him, set him apart. I put the piece of paper in my pocket and dumped out the vase of water into the sink. The daisy lay limply across the drain. I picked it up, removed the petals one by one and put them down the drain until it was just a stem with a yellow head. Then I tore the stem in two and tossed it in the wastebasket. I left in my costume to wait in the wings.

After playing "Freeze," after my stint on Jordan's knee, pretending to be a ventriloquist dummy, everyone clapped. I had jumped in, just like the others, taken a scene and changed it to what I wanted it to be. Jordan told us once how certain actors played parts, while others *became* their parts. "It's the difference between mediocrity and stardom," he said.

The cast liked our ventriloquist sketch so much, they decided to put it in the show. "Bravo," Bernice said. "Bellissima."

We practiced the sketch again, Jordan and I, to brainstorm lines. We hashed out details: drinking water, Jordan throwing his voice. It was high comedy. But I couldn't hold the dummy smile for long. "You'll have to do something about that," he said. So afterwards, I sat in front of the mirror looking at my face, forcing an exaggerated smile and opening my eyes wide. After thirty seconds, the edges of my mouth started to twitch. My eyes began to hurt. I held it longer: a minute, two. My jaw wobbled, my cheeks shook. My face no longer looked like a smile. Ridges appeared, wrinkles. Tears slid from my eyes. After ten minutes, my wooden composure had turned into a seeping, soft, dolorous face.

Every revue needs a can-can. We lined up for our own tailor-made bit of political satire, singing "In the Navy," replacing the word "Navy" with "Mounties." Mounties have a high profile in Fort Macleod, home of the Empress Theatre and the fort that the early Royal Canadian Mounted Police established to put an end to the whisky trade, something that they never truly accomplished. The cast, all white kids from the suburbs, locked their cars in the parking lot behind the Empress. In the middle of the day once, we were accosted by an Indian wanting change. Spray paint fanned from his nostril to his cheek. One time we found the window on the driver's side of Austin's car shattered in pieces, his stereo stolen. We reported the theft and comforted Austin. "It's okay," he said. "It's my dad's car."

We were high-kicking now. Ben strutted in front of us. He wore the same uniform: black pants with a yellow stripe, exaggerated saddlebags on the side, a red coat with brass buttons. But instead of our straight-brimmed porkpie hats, he sported a turban. Canada is a cultural mosaic, the turban implied. It will protect you, your religion, your freedoms. You can maintain your culture and still be a Mountie. We got to the chorus. "We want you as a new recruit," we sang. Our buckles gleamed in the lights, our leather boots clomped out the beat.

I went to the Salvation Army on the first Tuesday of the month, when they let you stuff anything you want in a bag for five bucks. The store was bustling with families, Hutterites, and farmers. My friend Steve was with me. He was also a thespian, having been in plays at Lethbridge Collegiate Institute. He'd been in *Harvey* and *Grease,* but only had bit parts. Steve hated secondhand shopping because he was so tall. None of the clothes fit. But I was medium-sized, with an average waistline, average shoe size, average height. At the checkout my bag was full.

"Aren't you in that show in Fort Macleod?" the lady behind the counter asked.

"Yes," I said. Steve nudged me. This seemed to happen to me a lot lately. The woman didn't ring up my bag.

"I want to thank you," she said. She had auburn hair with a tuft of grey at the crown, saucer-sized glasses with filigree hinges.

"For what?"

"I have a seven-year-old son who we've been trying to get to take music lessons. He has an ear for music, but he won't do a thing when we tell him to. But when he saw your fiddle number, he all of the sudden wanted to play the violin. 'I want to do that, Mom,' he said. Ever since then he's been taking lessons."

"Wow," I said.

She handed me my bagful of clothes. "Take it," she said.

"It's only five bucks," I said.

"That's okay," she said.

Outside, Steve turned to me and said, "Only you, Freeze."

My "fiddle number" was "The Devil Went Down to Georgia." I was the only violinist in the cast, so it was up to me to play both the Devil's and Johnny's parts. When I was the Devil, I slid a red headband with horns onto my head. I was lit up, the lights covered with red gels. As Johnny, I took off the headband and the light changed to white. On cue, I played the repetitive motif, complete with double stops and improvised flourishes. When the audience clapped, I tapped my feet on the blacktop in rhythm. When they didn't, I moved with the music, dipping the violin neck up and down and playing runs along the fingerboard.

"The Devil Went down to Georgia" was Carli's idea. A number where she could dance and they could use my talent on the violin. She interpreted the story with her body, sheathed in devil-red spandex. I accompanied on the violin, with our piano-effects guy on a portable Roland. It was a serious number. But after almost a month of watching Carli shimmy and jeté onstage, Jordan had had enough.

"Bad reviews," Jordan said one afternoon. He bought ten copies of the article. You could tell what the journalist thought by skimming the adjectives. "Brilliant" for Jordan, "endearing" for me, "nuanced" for Kelly, and "overzealous" for Carli and Bernice. Carli and Bernice were the directors and hadn't yet arrived.

"What do we do about it?" Sam said.

"I think they should be cut," Jordan said. Jordan was adept at passive voice. Decisions were made. That's how the show progressed.

"They're not that bad," I said.

"Carli is fat," Jordan said.

"You're so rude," Lynette said.

"She's a dancer. It looks ridiculous. And it's the only serious piece in the show. The audience never knows what to do."

Carli entered through the Empress's double doors wearing a bohemian skirt and a red beret. Fat? I hadn't thought of her as such.

"What's wrong?" she asked.

Jordan passed her a paper. I read over it while we waited for her to finish. "The two overzealous directors repeatedly interrupt the show's flow, culminating in a passé performance of the choreographer in an otherwise satisfactory 'Devil Went Down to Georgia.'"

"These reviews," she said, shaking the paper.

No one said a word.

"We think it's a little more than that," Jordan started. He explained how we had been getting reviews like this from other sources as well, and that when Mark Campbell came, he was fine with everything except the directors' bit parts to try to give the show narrative cohesion. "'It's improv,'" he quoted Mark as saying. "You have to maintain that energy." Carli nodded for a while until she realized how what he was saying implicated, or rather extricated her, then she said, "Hold it. If I'm right, you're telling me that you want me out."

"Not so bluntly, but yes."

Carli stormed out. On her way, she called Jordan conceited, reprehensible. When Bernice came in, they phoned

Beverley, the CEO of Star Singers, our producer. Beverley asked for Jordan to come on the line, to explain his side. They argued for an hour while we waited, listening to the cursing and cheap shots. That night, we replaced Carli with Kelly and Lynette who wore fishnet stockings and leather jackets, their '80s hair done up in red bandanas, sex props for the devil. The audience loved it.

After the number, Lynette complained about the push-up bra she had to wear during "The Devil Went Down to Georgia." It chafed her skin and made her boobs look too big.

"Why do women wear bras anyway?" I asked.

She stopped in the stairwell and Jordan caught up. "Because, dummy, if we didn't, our boobs would fall off."

"Very funny," I said.

"Look Jordan, he doesn't believe me."

"Some people never learn."

They pushed past me. Jordan had his hand on her back, like an usher. We were at the line of dressing rooms. "Could you help me out of this?" she asked. She took off her jacket, lifted up her hair and scrunched it against her head. The bra was black. They entered the dressing room and as I passed I heard them laughing.

Near the end of the summer, at a party, I skunked the mayor of Fort Macleod in a game of Ping-Pong.

"Nice forehand smash," he said. "Strong." He shook my hand like he was in a photo giving me a billboard check for a million dollars.

"Thanks," I said.

Bud Murray ran the Ford car lot until he had accumulated enough wealth to retire, then he worked as mayor. Every summer for Canada Day, he waxed his '57 Mustang convertible and rode it up and down Main Street, mere steps from the Empress entrance. He depended on attractions like our show for summer tourism dollars and this party was for us. That afternoon he played host on his estate just south of Fort Macleod, a corner lot in a gated community. He had a private pool, a barbecue, and a smoker. He insisted on cooking the meat himself, fending off jokes about leftover horse meat from the glue factory, one of Fort Macleod's main industries. I liked watching how Mayor Murray could work his guests. He had the infectious laugh of a politician and knew when to dig or tease, and when to lay off. He had seen the show seven times and talked with us after each performance. I went inside to get something to eat. Meat from the mayor's smoker sat in a stringy stack. I picked up a paper plate and scooped some of the meat onto a bun with a fork. I grabbed an orange pop and went outside to talk with Kelly and the mayor's wife.

"Did I ever tell you that you remind me of my nephew?" Mrs. Murray said.

She hadn't, but I wasn't surprised. Looking like someone else was part of being an actor.

"I don't think you have," I said.

"He's a regular comedian, just like yourself. Oh, he doesn't act *professionally* or anything, but he was Gilbert Blythe in *Anne of Green Gables*."

"Have him try out. He could be in the cast next year."

"Oh, you're so funny," she said.

Mayor Murray came over and removed a red-and-white apron. "This boy beat me in Ping-Pong," he said, "right in my own house."

"You're too good a host," I said. "You lost on purpose."

"I wouldn't think that," Mrs. Murray said. "Buddy takes his Ping-Pong very seriously."

"How about a rematch?" the mayor asked.

"Sure," I said.

The first game, the game I skunked him, we were almost alone in his downstairs family room. This time, his wife and Kelly followed us, as did other members of the cast: Jordan, Sam, and Lynette. We rallied for a bit and then started to play. Mayor Murray was keeping up. He held the paddle traditionally and he had a fierce backhand smash. But he had problems getting to the sides quickly enough; his girth made rounding the corners difficult, and most of the time he would just let the ball go rather than relinquish his dominant position behind the middle line. I played pen-style, with a weaker backhand, but, like he had already mentioned to me, a powerful forehand smash—almost unreturnable when it connected. But now my smash wasn't connecting with the same accuracy and we were nearing the end of the game. It was 19–16. I had a comfortable enough lead, but it was my serve and I was nervous.

The mayor was sweating under the armpits and his bald head beaded up. Practically the whole party was there. I netted my first serve. 19–17. "Don't give up now," the mayor said. He smiled, holding his paddle between both hands, waiting for the serve. I tried backspin to his forehand and he returned it with ease. I sliced sideways and the ball went down again to his forehand, bouncing off the side, too high. He reached over for it and hit it hard, straight down the side. I backed up, tried to side slice it again, but the return didn't reach the net. It was 19–18. I decided to dead hit it—no spin, and fast to his forehand. He was expecting spin and overcompensated, sending the ball too far and hitting me in the chest.

"Don't take it personal," I said. The mayor didn't smile this time. I threw the ball over to him for the game point. He backspun it to my forehand and I smashed it home.

The mayor congratulated me again but with not quite the same enthusiasm. "Twice in a row," he said. "That's what I like about you theatre people. Always have to be on your toes."

"Thanks," I said.

The mayor laughed. "You're a performer, all right. Hey, is it true what Jordan says? That you're just like your character in real life?"

The question caught me off guard. Jordan said that? Certain things, I suppose were similar–the joking around, the gullibility. But other aspects, like my character's struggle to understand even basic concepts, his mimicry of Jordan, and the forced confusion he felt were different. "I'm not sure," I said.

"Ha, ha," he said. "Yes, yes, that's right. Always on, I see. What a character."

He patted me on the back. I turned to the rest of the group to receive my congratulations.

It was the final curtain call. I was backstage. I had just changed out of my black pants from "The Devil Went Down to Georgia" and back into my dummy character's jeans and green T-shirt. Jordan was there. And Sam. Jordan was holding Sam's head with both hands and kissing his mouth.

"Just showing Sam how to stage-kiss," Jordan said. He smiled. Sam shifted his weight onto one foot, rocking away from Jordan. My pants hung on a nail and I reached for them, instinctively.

"Curtain call," I said. I took my jeans and left.

Now I waited behind the curtain as Bernice and Carli finished their short dialogue, praising, as they did every night, the show-within-a-show that we collectively produced.

"And that's show business!" Carli said. The music swelled and the audience clapped. Carli and Bernice parted for the wings. Kelly, next to me, said, "Where are they?" Jordan and Sam hadn't yet emerged from the basement. All of us were standing, hands locked, watching for their figures to come up the stairs. The curtain stayed down until I saw Sam's head. Both Sam and Jordan rushed for either side of the lineup and Jordan gave the signal for the curtain. The whole cast walked out together, stepped mid-stage, into the lights. Then each actor took two steps forward for applause, doing something in character. Sam struck a body-building pose, Kelly kissed her hand and waved, Lynette tap-danced. When it got to me, I walked out, as I always did, looking disoriented and confused. I turned in a circle, squinted at the audience and they clapped loudly. I saw a familiar head in the back, red hair bobbing up and down, holding her stomach as the laughter came rolling out.

POACHERS

In the fall of 1994, when I was 40, my twelve-year-old son Taylor shaved the neighbor's dog, the Dalmatian. My neighbor, Audrey, phoned to tell me. We hadn't talked to each other for years. Around lunch time, the Dalmatian streaked through our yard and the phone rang.

I was excited because Audrey was calling, on her own, all the way from across the street. I was hoping to hear that she had forgiven me at last. I had Taylor after an affair three years into my marriage to Ray, the man who Taylor believed to be his biological father. In a southern Alberta town of conservative Mormons, Taylor's birth made big headlines. I remember clearly his baby blessing, Ray holding him up in a white baby blanket, like an invitation to come see my son, the blue-eyed freak. I never could understand people's gradual rejection. I imagined myself becoming a spinster in my old age, my home a place where children would hate to walk past. "There she is," they'd say, eyeing my spinster silhouette, "The witch."

"He was laughing," Audrey said. She didn't have the gumption to criticize Taylor outright. I had to infer that his laughter was wrong.

"He's a child," I said.

"You really need to *do* something."

"I've seen worse." And I had.

"God help us," she said, and hung up.

In the last couple years Taylor had become increasingly reckless. When he was eleven, three neighbor kids witnessed Taylor lighting a batch of sticks next to the Coppins' garage. The Coppinses extinguished the fire before the whole building went up, but one side was charred in the shape of a fan. And a couple months ago, Taylor was caught shoplifting comic books from Jimmy's Convenience Store. He had to do a month of community service for that one, ruining, as he claimed, his entire summer. He'd become questioning and rebellious. Then a couple weeks ago, Taylor came home wanting to know about where his blue eyes came from, a question that Ray and I had staved off since his birth.

"Mom, am I adopted?" he asked.

"What?"

"Buddy Waldner says that I was probably adopted."

"You're not. You tell him you're not. Some kids think they know everything. Buddy's one of them."

"Are you sure?"

"Why, honey, why?" We were in the kitchen, just me and the kid. I looked through the cupboards to distract myself. The sound of opening and closing cupboard doors filled the space. I found an apple in the fridge, rattled the silverware drawer for a knife and cut myself some slices. "Here," I said. I cut out the core, handed Taylor some of my apple.

"Mrs. McDonald said that brown eyes are a dominant trait," Taylor said.

"Yes."

"But I have blue eyes. Dad has brown eyes."

"So what," I said. "You're not adopted." I had heard of instances where a recessive gene will manifest itself generations down the line—even to a family of all brown-eyed folks—though it was rare and unlikely. But I was sure he had to be from the affair, from Jack, a man whom I had met through my job as Ridgeview's economic development officer. The big clue: Jack had blue eyes, Ray had brown.

There were other indications of his parentage that were less obvious. He inherited Jack's delicate frame, for one thing, and he had the same small, flat teeth that looked ground down. I couldn't help but speculate about Taylor's emerging features and character. Would he end up like my husband Ray, a man governed by habit and religion? Or like Jack, an impulsive son of a bitch who promised me the world for a few months of escape?

"I'd be OK if I was adopted, you know. Some of my friends are. They even look a little like their parents. And we read this article in school about an adopted girl who found out she was a twin and now they're best friends."

"Well you're not. You don't have a twin."

"OK, don't freak out," Taylor said.

"I'm not freaking out."

I decided to push the science lesson. Tell him what I'd told him before, what he'd most likely told his friend Buddy. "And blue eyes are a recessive gene. Sometimes crops up. You just happened to get them."

"That's what I thought," he said. He seemed disappointed. I told him to come here and give me a hug, as though I felt he needed it. He was reluctant at first. I explained how genes work, how there were exceptions. Each sentence, to me, contributed to a very persuasive argument—so strong, I found myself wanting to believe it, to keep it that way, keep telling him over and over, reinforcing the lie. Worse things had been done to children, and some people would say that he didn't need to know. But I knew, even as I held him there, telling him that he wasn't adopted, that my little gnawing conscience would get the better of me.

So after the Dalmatian, after Audrey's phone call from across the street, I knew that it was time. I sent Taylor out to play, then called Ray at work—hoping to hear some confirmation or support for my resolution to tell Taylor about his paternity. All Ray said was "Are you sure? Sure sure?"

emphasizing the second "sure"–not the response that I'd hoped for. But I had decided. There was still toughness in me.

"The bastard probably already knows," I said. A joke. It hurt me to talk like this. I waited for Ray to respond, holding onto the phone like it was a hot iron that needed to be there. Did he not get it? I blurted out one heavy "hah," like a misdirected hiccup and broke out crying. He started to talk and it made me angry to hear him so sympathetic, like he wanted to hold my head in his hands, pat my back and say "There, there," like in a bad commercial.

"Audrey called me today," I said, still upset. I imagined Ray with the phone wedged between his shoulder and his ear while he ate his lunch.

"A surprise?"

"Taylor shaved their Dalmatian. She called to tell me."

"He did what?"

"He shaved it with the clippers. It looks like a pink Pinto."

"I'll be over in an hour." He hung up.

I decided to tidy up the house, get my mind off things. But everything seemed to reveal Taylor's recklessness: microwaved Legos, scattered loose leaf, comic books. I put doilies over the permanent marker on the coffee table, turned the couch cushions upside-down to conceal burn marks from Taylor's magnifying glass. Some things you can hide. Then there was a knock at the door.

"Audrey?"

If you were in the neighborhood, you might think that she was on her way to a business meeting: sensible pumps, grey skirt, cream blouse. Our yuppie neighbors. She was slim and fit and perfect, like one of those fake Christmas trees where all the limbs were symmetrical, and I wondered what someone so perfect was doing here, on my porch, breaking our truce of silence for the second time that day. "I thought you might want this," she said. "I know you love to read."

"Thanks," I said. She handed me a book and before I could glance at the cover, she'd left, striding across the street.

She had given me a "how to" book about raising kids by Dr. Laura. I flipped through the pages, skimmed the subject headings about being a role model, building moral character, and maintaining familial relations. I went upstairs and put it in the recycling bin. I knew what this book was about. I had already done everything wrong.

Ray came home a half hour later.

"Audrey is a priggish shit," I said.

"Take it easy," he said.

Ray paused for a second to give me space, then got out a stack of brochures and travel guides and spread them on the coffee table like in a hotel lobby. "I got these travel brochures from Gale. What do you think about taking a little weekend trip? We could tell Taylor then, just our family, up in the mountains somewhere."

I shook my head.

Ray said, "You know Taylor's going crazy because he's getting older. Puberty is setting in and he feels less obligated to behave. Out there, I could clear that up in a hurry."

Like Ray was some new-and-improved acne cream.

Ray kept talking in his objective tone, as though he were Taylor's child psychologist. Despite everything, Ray held to his nuclear family notions. When I first told him about the affair, I was sure that it would destroy us. I had already made plans to move to Lethbridge and live with my sister. But he insisted that he still loved me, that God would forgive me and that all our problems would be solved as long as we lived by the gospel and did everything together, as a family.

"This looks nice," I said, to stop the lecture. I was halfway into a brochure about Gargantua Caves.

"Gargantua is out," he said. "You'd need a lot of gear. It takes rappelling ropes to get down inside."

I sighed. "I have to do something."

"Maybe it could work," he said. "But only if we did just the main level. No one would be up this time of year."

Ray got out the topographical map to show me the route into Gargantua. The trailhead zigzagged up a steep gradient shown by the tight black lines. "It goes up, up, and up, waaaay up," he said, like the friendly giant on the TV show. Even from the map Gargantua looked huge.

"But how do we get *in* there," I asked.

Ray pointed to where you turned off Crowsnest. There was a gravel road, marked in blue, heading west into British Columbia. But the road kept going past the entrance to a valley, and past the trailhead he had just shown me. There was nothing–nothing but rivers and valley that marked the distance between the gravel road and the trailhead.

"And after that?" I asked.

"That's why we have a 4x4," he said.

I smiled. I imagined us riding a monster truck into the valley, cruising through the rivers and over gullies like they were junk cars, leaving tracks as wide as a house. Like we were going in to make a road, our tires spinning and spitting up mud and earth, carving a place for us in the landscape in the same way lovers carved their initials into trees. That's where we went, we'd say, look at that. Straight as an arrow through the heart.

"I'll think about it," I said.

The next day, the old sadness started coming back. I had felt this way several times after the affair, when I found myself pregnant and finally realized that Jack was a player. At first I couldn't bring myself to tell Ray about it. I still loved him. I took long secluded drives in the countryside, thinking about plowing into telephone poles. A favorite spot was the old make-out point at Ridge reservoir where teenagers would go on the weekend. You could see the whole reservoir from the point, the prairies and the foothills leading up to the grey-and-white line of the Rockies to the west. I rolled down the windows and locked the doors, made sure that my seatbelt was securely fastened. I wanted so badly to project myself into the water, car and all, and drown like an unwanted kitten. At times I felt that I would go through with it. But mostly, I just thought. I liked the shifty gravel roads and the dry solitude of the prairie—the feeling of speeding east with the wind, just right so that there was barely any resistance, like I was moving everywhere and nowhere all at once.

Then that weekend we were off to the mountains. Kananaskis country.

This is how it went: I continued taking long drives thinking of plowing into telephone poles while Ray packed. Ray thought of everything: plenty of socks, glimmering mess kits, travel alarms, freeze-dried food he picked up at Mountain Equipment Co-op in Calgary, and sleeping bags, tents, ground cover, all techno-fabrics, light as a dime. When Ray said to travel light, he meant to travel with gear that weighed less. Taylor went along reluctantly, wondering why, all of a sudden, his parents were ready to head for the hills together like Lewis and Clark. On the way up, Ray gave several lectures while I drove. He went over a list of things to do: find a spot under a tree, make sure to tie up the packs, don't build a fire. I was getting addled by his constant chatter, thinking all the time of the conversation that I had had with Ray the night before about when we would tell Taylor.

"When?" I asked.

"Whenever the time is right. You'll know when," he said.

Then I made the big mistake of fishing Audrey's book out of the recycling bin. What I needed was more definitive advice—a source that I could use to confirm my decision. But when I turned to the chapter, "Indiscretions" I was disappointed with what I found. Dr. Laura's tone was right—she used strong qualifiers like "always" and "never," superlatives like "best" or "least." I got to liking the clear line of reasoning, the almost acidic way she could put down words. I read the chapter twice, each time sweating through the whole thing, reading as though someone had a gun to my head saying "Read this. Now." And the advice was always the same, never wavering. Don't tell your kid you've done something wrong if it's no longer a problem. She used countless examples of parents sharing drug experiences or infidelities in ways that royally screwed up their kids' lives. I tried over and over again to justify my own approach, my need to share my thoughts with Taylor, to have it all out between us, but in truth I was just stigmatizing the whole situation. If Dr. Laura was right, my kid was headed for a pretty sucky life.

The rest of the morning, Ray rambled on about camp etiquette, all the way after the turn off Crowsnest and past the bumps and creek crossings. Finally, we got up to the trailhead. So much for being alone in the wilderness. A monster pickup was there, parked and empty.

"I thought you said no one would be up this time of year."

"Usually," Ray said.

I felt sick. For me, the deal was off. I couldn't talk to Taylor—not with other people around. And we were sure to meet them—there was only one trail, one campsite. My sorrow needed room. I could be one person in a huge crowd of people or a woman alone, but not this—one of two parties out in the middle of Kananaskis country. Someone had mapped the same spot, made the same plans, and that was enough to keep me from wanting to talk to my son.

We started the hike. Ray said he hoped that the people were friendly. Then he gave a great lecture about poachers. Poachers, he said, had no regard for rules, like cars on highways with no speed limits. He quoted scripture. "If you are willing and obedient, you will eat of the good of the land," he said. "If you refuse and rebel, you will be devoured with the sword." The trail got steeper. I imagined Ray being mangled by a bear.

About mid-way, I knew that we were scaling the compressed lines on Ray's topographical map. The pitch was steep and we were heading through shale. Each step slipped back half a stride. At a stump, Ray stopped and took off his pack. Taylor stuck out his arms and rotated them, and faked falling backwards as he sat down.

"Careful," I said.

Ray took out a canteen and downed a few gulps of water, then passed it around. I was speculating about the other group. Maybe they had gone somewhere else? Staked a claim in the valley? So far, we had just seen shale and scrub pine and no signs of people. Then Ray said, "Taylor, I bet you're wondering why we wanted to do this trip."

I shook my head. Not now. "Ray," I said.

"Because I'm in trouble?" Taylor said.

"Ray . . ."

"No, Taylor, you're not. Remember a while back when you asked your mother about being adopted?"

"Mom told you about that?"

Bastard. Bastard. Bastard.

"Yes, she did, Taylor. And I think that she has something else to tell you."

Taylor looked at me, surprised. I rubbed my shoulder with one hand. My shirt was damp where my pack straps had been. Ray came over, sat behind me on a boulder, then reached down to massage my back. I got up.

"Let's go for a walk, kiddo," I said.

I took Taylor by the elbow, the way I used to when he was naughty and I needed a corner to tuck him away. But we were going uphill, leaving Ray behind to guard our packs. Taylor kept up my pace for a while, then I let go of him when we reached a patch of shale and we both needed the space. Taylor said, "What's wrong, Mom? Why won't you tell me what's wrong?" repeatedly as we climbed until breathing from exertion broke up the sentences into fragments punctuated by more and more silence. I stopped at a tree in the trail that grew straight out of the limestone and then up, forming an elbow of a trunk.

"Here," I said. "Let's stop here."

Taylor hopped up on the ledge and put his arm along the trunk. I climbed up behind him and straddled him, wrapping my sweaty arms around him from behind. I was still almost a foot taller than my son, though I knew that wouldn't last. He was just starting puberty, or so he told me, and Jack had been tall and wiry, six-two or six-three. I found myself thinking about Jack's feet, the boat-shaped loafers that he commonly wore. Taylor's shoe size had changed three times in the past year and his runners were starting to get cramped again.

"How are your feet?" I asked.

"Cut it out, Mom. You're all sweaty and gross."

I pulled back and slid alongside him.

"When we get going down, you'll have to tie your shoes a little tighter. I don't want you jamming your toes in the front."

"Is that what you wanted to talk to me about?"

"No, it isn't," I said. "I want to talk to you about your father."

I expected to cry. Each time I had pictured the scene, the tears would be there, on the surface, ready to flow at the mildest suggestion. But there I was, dry-eyed, telling my life's history like I was some distant cousin who messed up. I told Taylor that he wasn't adopted, but that he had a different biological father who I had known for just a short time.

"That's where you get your blue eyes," I said.

I told Taylor how Ray and I had wanted to give him a stable home life, that the affair was my fault not his, and that he had always belonged to us and not anyone else. I told him about the joy it had been raising him, and that Ray and I had given him the best of ourselves. I told my son what I had learned from my relationships with both men:

that he, Taylor was the most important and valuable person in my life. I told him everything.

That was it.

When we came back, Ray was reading his Bible.

"I almost gave up on you two," he said.

"You lugged that all the way up here? I thought you were all concerned about weight," I said.

"Always room for the word of God. Hi Taylor."

Taylor grunted, then hoisted his pack around his shoulders, cinched up the straps and headed, sure-footed up the mountain. He was unusually quiet. I couldn't read him. Ray waited until Taylor was out of earshot, then asked, "How'd it go?"

"You're an asshole," I said.

It took me about 3000 vertical feet, three blisters, and a lot of grunting to cool off. Ray had no right to expose me like that. I thought how I could rewrite the book that Audrey had given me. It would be short, like a recipe. How to tell your son he's the product of an affair: *For BEST results, don't agree to spend a weekend in the wilderness, don't put yourself in an uncomfortable situation, and whatever you do, don't tell your son that he's a bastard until you're on your way home.* Sound advice.

Finally, we reached the plateau. A six foot cairn of stacked limestone marked the spot, as did a fire pit, two tents, and a row of packs strung between trees. But the camp was deserted. We unslung our packs and sat on a log.

"I got to take a leak," Taylor said.

"Be careful."

And I meant it. From the plateau where we were, Turtle Mountain was still shedding its stone face. Shale and rock abounded, as did sink holes and gullies. The terrain was wildly unpredictable and I didn't want my son—my only son—going and peeing off some cliff like men like to do. Wouldn't that be the final irony—dragging him all the way up here and then having some horrible accident that maimed him for life? We didn't need any more scars.

So when I heard Taylor yell, "Helloooo," I jumped.

We heard voices responding to him, yelling back. He had found people. Ray and I followed in the direction that Taylor went, down through the rock-strewn vegetation to an area that spanned a long sweep of shale. The group, as we could see now, was made up of boy scouts, Venturers probably, who had a bunch of ropes slung around a tree. Extensive rappelling equipment. The boys were taking turns descending over the lip of the natural limestone bridge and down into the mouth of a cave that swallowed the shale.

"These guys are going *through* the caves," Taylor said.

The Venturer leader was a short, skinny man wearing an Aussie leather hat. He was mild-mannered and calm—not at all the kind of person I pictured leading a group of adventure-sprung teenagers into the backcountry.

"I'm Jake Duggan," the man said.

We introduced ourselves.

"A great idea, taking your son up here," Jake said. "This is the best time of the year. Less crowded." He talked quickly enough, but mumbled his words.

"But not this weekend," I said.

"You'd be surprised. During the summer, we get four, five groups at a time."

The boys rappelled and ascended on the rope. For long intervals, no one really talked. We just watched, arms folded, from a safe distance as the boys struggled on the rope, pulling an ascender attached to their foot up until their leg was cocked at a 90 degree angle, then standing and moving the ascender attached to their harness. One scout belayed for security. The whole system ran like clockwork with the ascender moving to the belay, then the belay descending, then the descender switching to holding the rope steady at the bottom. Some scouts took longer coming up and let their feet dangle in the air. Some moved as swiftly as though they were climbing a ladder. But whatever speed they went, it always looked like work.

"Can I try, Mom?"

Taylor was earnest and Jake seemed to know what he was doing, so we consented. Big mistake. The scouts were eager to show us how to use the equipment and they eventually conned us both into trying–Ray going down in one sliding jump and me taking my time in increments, letting the rope tighten and then slack. Before we knew it, the troop had invited us along.

That night, I went to bed early. Taylor and Ray stayed out with the scouts for a campfire while I found the solace of my sleeping bag. I got myself completely ready on my side of the tent, with ample room for Taylor next to me and Ray on the other side. I was idly hoping that Taylor would come to bed early, of his own volition, so that we could have time to talk. The rest of the evening completely derailed me, and I felt ousted by the Venturers' plans to go through Gargantua the next morning. Jake had showed us maps of the five rappelling pitches that led through a complex maze of tunnels and rooms. In places, the caves were like worm holes just six feet high, almost perfectly symmetrical with sandy bottoms. Interesting, sure. But the more Taylor latched on to what Jake was saying, the more I wanted to take my son back down to the trailhead, to the car, on to more familiar signs of civilization.

"Pam?" Ray unzipped the tent.

"Where's Taylor?"

"Smores. He'll come in a while."

I rolled over with my back to the center of the tent. I breathed slowly, like I had been sleeping. Ray kicked off his shoes and slid quietly into his bag. He rustled around for a bit, then stopped.

"I'm sorry, Pam."

"For what?"

"For bringing you up here. I didn't know there'd be people. I don't want this to turn into some scouting trip."

I didn't say anything.

"You two need time to talk things out."

No kidding.

"Why don't you both stay back tomorrow? I'll go with Jake and give him a chance to play tour guide. There's plenty to explore around the plateau."

"Maybe," I said.

I kept to my side of the tent and Ray sighed. He moved some more until I couldn't hear much of anything except the dull chatter of the scouts at the campfire and the wind coming up from the valley. I was still awake when Taylor crept into the tent. He smelled like wood smoke, earth, and pine. Then I went to sleep.

The next morning, I woke up before anyone else. I moved very slightly and positioned myself so that I could see Taylor clearly. Ray lay on the other side of the tent with his back to the both of us. He had always been a sound sleeper. Silent, never budged. Ray was great for things like that. He was always organized and dependable; he did dishes, kept his shoes on a shoe tree, always pressed his slacks. But love for him was overbearance. Had I been a different woman, I imagine that we could have had a happy life together. Me, Ray the forgiver, and our bastard son Taylor. One damn happy nuclear family.

"Taylor," I said as he was getting up, "I was wondering if you would stay back with me today."

"We're going to Gargantua."

"The scouts are going to Gargantua. I think that Dad might go too. But I want you to stay here with me."

"Why?"

Ray was awake now, calmly stretching, sitting up.

"I want us to have some time together to talk about yesterday."

"We already talked about it."

"Not really."

"What more is there?" he asked.

"Nothing more."

"Taylor," Ray said, "I think what your mother means is that she'd like to be alone with you in case you have something to say."

"Ray, I can handle this."

"This sucks," Taylor said.

"What was that?" I didn't like the word suck. Taylor knew it.

"This whole thing. The trip, your lying to me. It all sucks. Now I finally find something worth doing up here and you don't want me to go. Instead I have to stay back with my sucky mother in the sucky wilderness while my sucky father who isn't really my father goes up the mountain with the sucky Venturers. It's not fair. It sucks."

It was the most Taylor had said to me the whole trip. A real breakthrough. Ray started to laugh.

"Shut up," Taylor said. Ray laughed harder. "Will you tell him to shut the fuck up?"

That did a number on Ray's evangelical ears. I could see him gearing up for a lecture, so I cut him short. "That's enough, Taylor," I said. "You're staying with me this morning and that's final."

Another line I would add to my handbook: *Don't force your bastard son to stay with you so you can brood and feel sorry for yourself while the rest of the world goes on a spelunking adventure.* I thought about this over our re-hydrating peaches-and-cream mush. Ray was so ticked off that he ate his too quickly and burned his tongue. After breakfast, Taylor asked to go on a walk and I told him that he could if it wasn't far. He chucked the rest of his mush into the fire pit and ran off while the Venturers gathered up their gear.

"Is Taylor coming?" It was a short, skinny kid with a coil of ropes around his neck.

"We'll try to catch up," I said.

The Venturers followed the cairns up to a shale trail that cut like a scar across the face of the mountain. I watched them for a good twenty minutes before Taylor came back with his hands cupped together.

"That must have been some pee," I said.

"I found a toad."

"Toads don't live up this high."

"What's this then?" Taylor brought his hands up to my face and opened them, slowly. It was a toad all right. I flinched and the toad hopped into my lap, then onto the ground. We both watched it as it shuffle-hopped into some unseen crevice under a log.

"How about that," I said.

"You'll tell the guys you saw it?"

"Sure I will," I said. Taylor sat down next to me. "You in the mood for a hike?"

"Sure."

I gathered up some gear: a couple flashlights with extra batteries, our helmets, and some trail mix. I made sure we had coats and that we both had jeans and gloves. I led the way, following the cairns that dotted the limestone plateau. My intention at this point wasn't quite clear. Another Dr. Laura no-no. I had no plan, no direction, and we were both inexperienced spelunkers wandering around a plateau filled with gullies and sinkholes. We made our way over to a green swath of water and moss with spikes of bear grass poking through the rock. I marveled at the way the mountain gave way, almost reluctantly, to bits of life. Here there were still late-blooming wildflowers, bees.

"Where are we going?" Taylor asked.

"I thought we could do some exploring. Maybe make it up to the glacier and slide down."

We hiked in silence for a while. I wanted to talk. At first I thought I'd better not. I didn't want to do the same dumb move that Ray did yesterday, unnaturally exposing a wound. This weekend, it was like both Ray and I were boxers, darting around Taylor in the ring, his eyes closing up, wanting his manager to cut them so he could finish. There was something hurtful about the whole thing, like he had been our little experiment over the last twelve years of his life. Like the Dalmatian, but bigger. I feared that he would get in some accident or hurt himself through his own mischief. His death could confirm so many things. But here he was, alive as ever, waiting for me to prod him again with questions.

"I want to talk to you, Taylor, but I'm not exactly sure what to say. About yesterday. The whole thing."

Taylor kept walking, then sighed and stopped as though he had expected it. "OK. Shoot."

Shoot, I thought. He said *shoot.* It wasn't right. My timing was off. In a few years, a few months, a few weeks, maybe. Not now. "You don't want to," I said. Damn. Now I sounded hurt.

"It's fine, mom. Really. I'm twelve."

"What an indictment," I said.

"What?" Taylor said.

Fine. "How about you ask me questions?" I said.

"OK," he said. "Why did you take us up here?"

"To talk to you."

"You could talk to me at home."

"I thought here would be better."

"Why?"

"Because there wouldn't be any distractions. No one else around. Ray said we would bond. You know, like a family. Beaver Cleaver and all that."

"Who?" he said.

"Never mind," I said. Up near the saddle, we could see the line of Venturers, cutting their way across. "I just thought it would be good to do something together. So you would know that you could come to us with any problems."

"What, like I don't come to you with my problems already?"

"That's not what I meant."

"So what did you mean then?"

"That we know what it's like. We were kids once too."

"Hah." Taylor said. Not a laugh, just the word. "Sure you do. You know real well."

"Regardless of what you may think, we care about you Taylor. We planned this whole trip for you."

"No you didn't. You planned it for yourself."

I didn't know what to say to that. A kid can change your perceptions about everything in an instant, like Taylor shaving that dog, turning simple black and white to shades of grey and pink. Now I found myself suggesting that we catch up with the Venturers, realizing that had been my intent from the beginning. We picked our way through the rocks, moving swiftly, commenting only on the contours of the limestone, the saddle scraped clean by melting snow. When Taylor did talk again, he was less abrasive, like my son when he was seven or eight and more obedient. But I didn't want to talk. Instead I stared at the steep drop to our left and looked for the cairns, lining them up like beacons. Was this trip, as Taylor suggested, just self-indulgence? I found myself thinking of an old friend, Angela, who had died from an overdose on anti-depressants. I remembered seeing her once in Fraser Foods, fingering through the lettuce, moving back and forth from head lettuce to leaf lettuce, just standing there in the aisle. I knew what she was thinking–head lettuce lasts longer, but doesn't taste right. Head lettuce is more economical, leaf lettuce healthier. The sadness was there as plain as the faces of her two teenaged sons, her 3-bedroom bungalow, her husband. Was her drug self-indulgence? When she died, I felt the same sadness for her that I had felt sitting behind the steering wheel, wanting to hurl myself into a brick wall.

We reached the mouth of Gargantua, a giant gopher burrow in the side of the mountain. The scouts were already on their way into the cave, but they stopped when they saw us coming.

"Decided to join us?" Jake asked when we clambered up to the mouth.

"Couldn't bear to stay away," I said.

Ray was smart enough not to say anything. We would talk about it when we were home tomorrow night, lying in bed with the lights off. I quickly changed into my coat and told Taylor to do the same. We duct-taped our flashlights to our helmets and followed the scouts into the cave.

I'm not sure when the transition happened, but Taylor started hanging back with me. I don't know why. Perhaps he sensed that I was upset. Even so, I didn't think he'd prefer my company to the Venturers, but there he was. After the first pitch, Taylor waited until I'd made my way down the rope, then he helped me off. I followed Taylor until we came to a room with an almost flat eight-foot ceiling. Jake was waiting for us. "This room lies between both provinces," he said. He made all of us turn off our lights and we stared into the dark and listened to the sounds of the cave. Gradually people's lights blinked on, the room sliced by rays of light. I flashed mine down at Taylor who was nibbling on some trail mix. He picked through, neglecting the raisins. By now, most everyone had left, their lights dimming in the distance. Taylor got up and I put my hand on his shoulder. "Let's sit here for a while," I said.

"OK."

Instinctively, we both turned off our lights. I listened to Taylor's breathing, the dull crunching sound of his teeth on the trail mix.

"Come here," I said.

Taylor responded and came close to me, resting between the crook of my arm and my breast like a lover. Taylor grabbed my other hand and held it straight up, spreading my gloved fingers in front of us. In my mind I superimposed the image of my hand, slender, nails painted, over the blank space. It was Taylor who broke the silence. "Mom," he asked. "How did you and Dad meet?"

"Ray? I don't know. There's not much to tell." Taylor kept asking me, going through every cliché in the book: did he sweep you off your feet? Was it love at first sight? I realized that I had never really told him these things. It had always seemed so drab and normal. So I told him. "I met him at school, when I was just finishing my degree. We dated for a while, then he asked me to marry him."

Taylor wanted to know details.

"We just decided is all. He seemed to think that it was a good idea and I believed him."

Taylor let this sink in. "So how did he do it? Did he get down on one knee? Did he take you someplace romantic?"

"You're still too young to be worrying about romance," I said.

"So did he?"

"No. It was like I said. We decided that it was a good idea. I don't even remember where we were."

I sat up and turned on my light. It was already getting weak. Talking about Ray made me uncomfortable, but if there was a time to tell him, to talk to him about our relationship, it was now.

"So do you love him?"

I fumbled through my pack for some batteries.

"Do you love Dad?"

I clicked my light off, unscrewed the back, slid the old batteries out and put them in my pocket. I reached for Taylor in the dark, felt for the down-filled sleeve of his jacket. "I don't know, honey," I said.

A beam of light licked the corners of the room, lighting them up briefly, then moved elsewhere along the wall.

"Hello?" It was Ray.

"Wait," I said. I put the new batteries in and we turned on our lights.

"Hey," Ray said. He kicked a piece of shale. "We thought you were lost."

"Just resting," I said.

"Oh."

Ray stood there, the obvious outsider, while Taylor and I struggled up and sat on the rock. I wanted to feel anger at the interruption, but couldn't find the spark. If the room we were in could hold two provinces, it could handle one dysfunctional family. The last chapter in my own self-help book would be: *Don't go spelunking if you're claustrophobic.*

Finally, Taylor asked, "Dad, who is Beaver Cleaver?" Ray laughed. "You are, Taylor" he said. "You're the Beav."

GOTHS

The boy had a ring on his thumb. It was silver, with a knob on one end like the head of a serpent. He had purple nails. *Purple.* Pauley didn't know if he'd ever seen purple nails on a boy, only in those shows that his daughter watched sometimes when she thought her parents weren't looking: MTV or that VHS or whatever station where they played music and singers sort of wormed their way around the screen looking in the camera with their eyes down like they had a secret or were about to take off their clothes or drive a shiv into you, take your pick. Pauley wondered if these kids would drive a shiv into him, were the kinds of kids who had shivs, made Molotov cocktails, kids who burned things or stapled cats to walls.

"You want to go in? It's almost over. There's just twenty minutes left." Pauley was talking but the kid put his hands in his back pockets, like he was feeling for something and his friend, another lean, sick-looking smoker with pants down to his knees and a silver chain looped between pockets, was already scoping the dance, looking through the lobby of the Ridgeview Stake Center social hall to the gymnasium where teenagers gyrated to some song about how you have to groove or have groove, a strange word "groove" like "groovy" from Pauley's childhood that nobody ever used anymore, a word that he hoped didn't mean sex or female genitalia or anything perverted or sexual or nasty because it was a popular song and kids had

been requesting it all night and Pauley didn't want to have
to change the music again just because the lyrics were sug-
gestive. Taylor was on the mixing machine and he knew
the rules.

The long-haired kid pulled a wallet out of his back
pocket and palmed two bucks into Pauley's outstretched
hand. Pauley said, "OK, but you're going to have to wear
these." He kicked a corrugated box of ties out from under
the table. The ties were tangled together, creased and
twisted in paisley knots. What would these kids—what was
it they called them nowadays? Goths?—think of Pauley's
batch of 70s paisley? Pauley waited for the inevitable
cringe, the way most kids held up one of the ties like it was
a soiled diaper. This was his dunce cap for those who forgot that this was a Mormon youth dance. Kids only 14-18,
dresses for the girls, shirts and ties for the boys. Pauley
knew the rules were unpopular—how many times had he
argued with the dance committee about it? But rules kept
out the trash and everything he associated with them:
drugs, alcohol, smoking, sex, and fights. But these Goths
didn't seem put off. One, the smoker with pants down to
his knees and bang-less hair that sort of swallowed his face
in ratted, half-curls, said "these are awesome" and pulled
one tie out of the pile, wide as a dinner napkin, made of
coarse polyester. Thin green, peach, and blue lines striped
a yellow background between paisleys the size of hum-
mingbirds. The boy tied the paisley wonder in a granny
knot until Pauley tut-tutted him and showed him how to
do it right: a half-windsor with the tip where the top of the
boy's pants should have been. The purple-nailed boy followed suit, both of them laughing, the ties a joke now, a
necessary accessory, and the boy with the hair pointed his
finger to the ceiling and then down and he swung his hips
south like that movie *Saturday Night Fever* and the boys'
girl—she was with either or both, Pauley couldn't be sure—
laughed and clapped her hands and managed to jump
even though her black boots looked like they weighed as

much as she did. And now the Goths were getting ready to go in the door for the last fifteen minutes of the dance and Pauley didn't know what to do.

Pauley said, "No head banging in there."

"Head banging?"

Pauley wasn't sure that's what they called it. He wanted only to describe the 80s, the metal bands, when they moved their heads so that their hair flung wildly about. This kid had long hair—the purple-nailed kid's hair was fine but messy and the girl's hair was boy short and she wore what qualified as a dress even though he knew the boots would make a racket on the maple floors—and he didn't want him making any more of a scene. Maybe he could hold him back from entering the dance on account of his hair? "You have to tie your hair back," Pauley said. "With this."

"Sure thing, man. You got it." The kid took the elastic and pulled his hair into a ponytail. The official rules didn't have anything specifically about hair, but Pauley made a mental note to change that: *no extreme hairstyles*. He watched the kids go in then sat back on the orange plastic chair. Having these Goths at large in the building made Pauley nervous. Where did these kids come from anyway? He'd seen that movie with the Goths a while back, much too violent. Probably suburban kids from parents too bored and lonely to care about them. What if there was something he hadn't checked for? An elastic certainly wasn't a barometer for a person's character. It wasn't a breathalyzer, couldn't detect drugs in their veins. Kids like these didn't come to church dances unless they were looking for trouble.

Inside the dance Taylor was playing a slow song, something whispery, no hint of any real vocals. Pauley wondered how the heck you could dance to the thing. There was no beat. Not like in the seventies when you knew just when to move your feet, when to jump, turn, swing your partner in and out. Fun music, not like this weepy teen garbage. But it had passed all the tests: it had acceptable lyrics, no harsh, violent beat, no innuendo. Just the wisp of a melody and a slow throbbing that made you want to lie down and let all life pass out of you. It took Pauley a while to locate the Goths. The new kid, Ponytail, was there dancing with the girl, slow-like, not really moving. A lick of his hair had escaped from the rubber band and divided his face in two. Pauley hadn't got much of a look at the girl, but now he could see her clearly—short boyish hair parted just off center, no bangs, her hair dyed a dark color. Just the kind of thing you'd expect this guy's girl to do—cut her hair short so that he could grow his long. Her dress was more like a black sack that went right to her knees. And those boots! Laces criss-crossed their way up her shins, just below her knees so that the only skin showing, besides her hands and face, were the small knobs of her kneecaps. The Goths teetered together like they were rocking with the pitch of a boat. The girl had her hands deep in the boy's back pockets, pushing his pants down even further so that his shirt came untucked and revealed the dark elastic of his briefs. Pauley clomped his way onto the dance floor and couples parted, giving him a wide berth.

"You can't do that in here."

"Do what?"

"You have to be at least a Bible's width apart."

"Sorry?"

Pauley pushed his hands in between the couple. He wasn't careful. Point was, the kids needed to stop being human blobs. They were supposed to *dance*—not this vertical petting, this prelude to sex. As he pushed in between them, he felt the boy's bony ribcage and the soft cup of the girl's breast. The girl said, "Hey!" and Pauley immediately withdrew his hands, shocked. Ponytail's hands were up in the air and the couple looked upset or confused or both. Pauley was embarrassed—he hadn't meant to touch the girl; she was shorter than he thought. They really should have moved when he first asked them, so he didn't have to use force. Maybe he should have pulled them apart by the shoulders? The couple went back to their bear-hugging stance and Pauley said "No. Like this." He brought over a nearby couple of fourteen-year-olds, a boy, barely pubescent, holding his hand high on the back of a statuesque brunette. Put the boy on her toes and she could've waltzed him around the room. "Like them. One hand together, the other on her waist. Yours on his shoulder." This time, results: the Goth and his girl, formal slow-dancing a Bible-width's apart, stiff and jerky as stop-motion photography. "Much better," Pauley said, noting, on the way out, Pony-tail with his cheek against his girl's, hands jutting forward like they were aiming a handgun together in a mock tango. So it was another joke. Pauley could handle that. Just as long as the girl wasn't grabbing Ponytail's butt.

Back in the entryway, Pauley pushed back in the orange plastic chair and dangled his legs and massaged the meat of his hand, trying to forget the softness of the girl's breast or the embarrassment afterward, that feeling of having really bungled something or making himself out to be squarer-than-square, an old man who just didn't know or understand what kids were about these days. He wondered if he'd been too suspecting, too judgmental. The kids were definitely not Mormon, he could tell that. It was mostly their smell, a stale smoke-and-cologne smell that belied both smoking and the habit of covering it up. Reminded Pauley of a Bishop he knew when he had been a missionary in North Carolina. He said that the best smell in church was of stale cigarettes, which was funny for a church that didn't condone smoking. What he meant was: we're getting in our doors the people who need our message. They are the people who are going to change. Now Pauley thought that he should have debriefed the Goths when they came in so that there wasn't any confusion, so that he didn't accidentally touch the girl's breast or make them feel unwelcome or uncomfortable, more conspicuous than they already were. When in Rome, do as the Romans. That was it. He had failed as a Roman guide. No wonder it was a joke–the Goths and the Romans. He looked at his box of wilted ties. Pathetic.

He would make it up to them. Maybe near the end of the dance, he could try to pass something off as an apology. He'd heard a statistic for conversion once from a friend of his who said that southern Alberta was one of the highest baptizing areas in North America. Astonishing, he had thought. How did it happen? Through the kids, the youth, at events like these. All people needed was a non-threatening environment and they would open up, bloom like spiritual flowers. He could say something, perhaps, thank everyone for coming in a way that implied recognition for the Goths, who had made the night unique. Maybe it would be best not to single them out publicly, but take Ponytail aside, just explain to him that he didn't mean anything by the ties or the bear-hugging. It's our culture, the way that Mormons show respect for our bodies, for each other. It's a form of veneration. But he wouldn't use that word, something simpler: *worship.* Pauley rubbed his hands on his khakis, slapped the fabric, felt the twinge of his muscles still just a touch sore from his run this morning.

Inside, another slow song. One more after this would signal the end of the dance and then the lights would come on, all the groomed Mormon youth in their seersucker dresses and cotton trousers blinking like they'd emerged from a cave. What were once cliques or groups or couples would now be just a big gymnasium with people, simple as the gleaming maple floors. But for now the youth had the cover of dark, each couple barely distinct in their mock-ballroom embraces. This time, he looked for the girl in black, her ponytail suitor leading her through the swells of dancers in a tango. He hoped they'd learned the correct behavior, now that they weren't necking on the dance floor, hormones flying everywhere. But he was chagrined not to find either. He looked again. There was Taylor at the mixing board, his head down, nimble fingers sliding a CD into a plastic sleeve, the stack of electronic equipment and wires taped to the floor, twirling youth, the smell of dirty perfume, and the implacable wall flowers. There were scuffs and the singular wail of an electric guitar accompanying some song about unrequited love. But no Goths. It was unnerving. As far as he knew, there was only the front exit that wasn't locked. Could the Goths have left the building?

Pauley walked to the center of the room. Kids parted to make way. No one was bear-hugging now. There couldn't have been more than eighty people at the dance and three kids with outlandish hairstyles didn't disappear that easily. He would have to search the rooms next, try to find where they were hiding out. He had found kids before in the bathroom, girls depressed that a boy had broken up with them or groups of kids sitting in the hall-way with their backs to the air conditioning vent if they'd been really dancing. Maybe they were on the stage? He had his answer soon enough. It didn't happen at the end of the song like some elaborate punctuation. It was mid-song, mid-sentence, mid-everything. A ringing like a recess bell, only louder, omnipresent. Some bozo had pulled the fire alarm.

Ponytail.

It was still dark but Pauley didn't wait. He shouldered his way through the circle of kids, their collective mum-bling and confusion adding to his ire. It was an indecent thing the Goths had done, cowardly. Pauley broke through the kids and sprinted for the foyer in time to see the pneu-matic hinge of the front door slowly letting the door click into place. Through the pale glass, he could see Ponytail and his friends, chains jangling, their loose clothing slap-ping around their skinny legs. Pauley punched the door handle and made for them like a linebacker ready to sack the quarterback. The Goths saw him, took off, ran. Was that profanity Pauley heard? They cut across the lawn, heading, he figured, to their car, their Goth getaway car. Pauley was pumping hard and gaining. If they stopped now, he'd have them. Just the time to open the doors and start the car would be enough. But instead, the kids swung left, down the street towards town. Fine. Pauley didn't mind a little jog.

The Goths weren't keeping good pace, kept looking back and then speeding up, like they couldn't believe that this guy was still after them. Old didn't mean you couldn't run. Pauley trained for chances like these, ran every morning religiously, even in twenty below weather, with a wind chill. The kids could sprint ahead, keep out of reach for a while, but Pauley was already pacing himself, just out for his daily jaunt, keeping his sights on his prey, waiting for them to tire. The Goths turned right onto Main, past Fraser Foods and Prairie Title. They rounded the corner at the Pharmacy and tried to ditch Pauley before Ridgeview Elementary, going left again down the gravel alley. But Pauley stopped, heard the crunch of their feet and tailed them, winding through the alley and tennis courts and the playground with the metal merry-go-round, the turtle-shaped monkey bars, the rooster with a seat on a spring. He didn't expect them to go much longer. The girl was lagging. They passed Ridgeview High, climbed the wire fence onto the football field, where the girl collapsed, lay down with her arms outstretched, like she was getting ready to do snow angels. Pauley paused, said "you're hanging out with the wrong people" but he couldn't stop. He was following the boy with the hair–the boy whose ponytail had fallen out and now was swishing to either side as he sprinted once more. The Goths cleared the north fence and Pauley followed; he climbed methodically, but his pants caught on a barb and ripped a fist-sized hole. Then they turned and headed straight through the town, past the copper awning of Demler's Ice Cream Parlor and down Baker Street, turned right past Jim Harlan's auto body shop and the Texaco before Highway 52. They'd gone a

good mile now, and the Goths didn't show signs of tiring.
Did they even know where they were going? Every so
often, Ponytail would slow to a walk, then he'd flip his hair
to the side and glance back. Soon they would be off again
in another direction at a dead sprint. The Goths were skit-
tish, Pauley could see that. They could sprint and walk and
sprint all they wanted, fartleks all the way to their destina-
tion, but he wouldn't let up.

Pauley heard the sirens after they'd been out a couple
miles. The Goths weren't sprinting anymore, were puffing
their cheeks, in and out, rhythmic. They turned right past
Doc Bernard's brick ranch and the old Chevy carcasses at
the Coulters', skirting the edge of town. They were on
gravel now and each step sounded like a dropping bean
bag. The Goths sure-footed it, barely eking out a 50-foot
lead. Pauley didn't close the gap. He wasn't angry now,
just confused. The fire trucks would be at the Stake Center
now, men in yellow hats mingling with a bunch of confused Mormon kids, checking the exits, turning off the
alarm. And where was he? Out in the sticks running down
a couple of Goths with paisley ties. Made him want to lean
over and belly laugh. Or catch those kids and tighten the
paisley beauts until the kids' heads popped like zits.

At the end of Baker Street, the boys disappeared.
Pauley's legs burned with lactic acid but his breath was still
sure; he had miles left in him. Overgrown junipers
crowded either side of the street and he listened for heavy
breathing, the sound of footfalls through the brush. A
shortcut. He could see where they went now, a thin line
beaten down in the earth like a deer trail. He dove
between the junipers and followed the meandering trail
until it broke on someone's back yard and he could see
Ponytail and his friend hoofing it past the weathered cedar
sign for Elsinore Estates.

So that was it, he thought. Not Goths, not yuppie
rebels, not even city slickers, but Ridgeview's own trailer
trash. Pauley sprinted into the estates. Past the line of

industrial mailboxes was a park with a jungle gym made out of used tires. The Goths hurdled a couple, making a bee-line for the other side. Pauley had never been in the trailer park before, except to visit old Madge Halpern before she passed away last spring. This was a dismal place to live. Old trailers with drooping aluminum awnings sat like great beached whales praying to an elephantine structure of radials and steel in the center, a kind of post-apocalyptic trailer-henge. The boys clambered up the stairs to a white trailer with vinyl siding, a little newer than the rest. Its one bay window made it look less like a barge and more like a manufactured wing of one of those plastic suburbia McMansions. The house looked clean, the gravel driveway new, and the spare décor decidedly un-Goth. It was plebeian and somehow hopeful. Upwardly-mobile Goths. Fiscally-prudent Goths. Light from the trailer filtered through the slatted blinds until someone winked them shut. Pauley stopped on the road, wondering what he was doing.

There was a lesson here. Some loaf-and-fishes miracle, devils cast out of swine. It was in the ties, or the chase. Every metaphor he tried seemed absurd, incongruous, and he felt suddenly on display, self-conscious of the sweat dampening under the arms, in the small of his back. His torn trousers. Pauley saw himself as a kind of wild man, the linebacker who wasn't afraid to hit all out, the good shepherd after his one sheep. A couple kids came into a dance, mocked him, took his paisley ties, pulled a fire alarm, and he chased them down to this place, this trailer park on the edge of his town. But the story lacked an ending. There was no moral. He wanted that conversation with the boys about stopping smoking; he would tighten the ties until it constricted their throats. "That's what it'll feel like if you're still breathing at forty," he'd say. Or even a hand through one of the vinyl windows, dropping the ties onto the fresh gravel would do it. Or the Goths apologizing, doing community service, the chase a joke they could count on after the Goths got city jobs or went to university. They would punch his arm, "You sure can run grandpa" and he'd jab back and they'd wrestle like a bunch of turkey-stuffed cousins playing Thanksgiving football.

He needed an answer. Pauley stepped on the gravel. His feet sounded on the hollow deck. He stood square as the door, reached up his arm. Waited for that solid knock.

A Prayer for the Cosmos

The spring the Cosmos won provincials, my brother-in-law Patrick, also my next-door neighbor, picked up a Mastiff/Lab mix from the pound and brought him home. The dog was good-natured, obedient, and square-headed, with a penchant for rawhide bordering on obsession. And he was young, plenty of energy. My wife, Audrey, and I were ecstatic. We owned a Dalmatian.

Our dog, Zeke, took an amorous liking to Otis, even though both the dogs were male and neither fixed. The first weekend we dog-sat, they exhausted themselves so much that Zeke slept for three days straight. Then we started to notice Zeke's neck. Bullet-sized welts, scabs. We didn't think much of it. The next time, I watched Otis clamp his mastiff-sized jaws onto Zeke's neck when they played. Once Zeke squeaked like a mouse. Otis didn't know the difference between a gummy chomp and a bite that'd take your head off.

Finally, I told Patrick about it.

"What's the trouble?" he asked. He started humph-humphing, a sort of stunted laugh.

I told him: the welts, Otis' play bites, how Patrick would have to take his dog to a kennel from now on.

"What about this weekend? It's too late to call the kennels. If you want, I'll just leave him at my place and you can check on him," he said when I'd finished. I waited for him to say something else, maybe to apologize, but he didn't.

"I suppose we could," I said. "But it's the last time."

"Good. It's settled then." Then he closed the door and he left me there on his porch like he had meetings to go to. End of discussion. I heard the lid of his piano knock open and Patrick going at some show tunes with gusto. I thought about changing my mind. We were planning a trip in June after school got out and we hated having to take our dog to a kennel. But I had said my piece, so I left.

Patrick was from Louisiana. He met my sister when a traveling group of singers from the University of Arizona came through Lethbridge. My buddies and I made fun of the show even though we went and paid real money for tickets at the Yates. They had one song where the cast was dancing and smiling like they were all on a helium high. Nice, prudish fun. The kids looked like something off a soap commercial. Zestfully clean. My sister Betty loved it. After the show, they had interviews for recruits and she signed on for a year after high school. She traveled all over the world and met diplomats and students from Great Britain to Alaska. But then she ended up with some swamp-hopper from Louisiana who was in the cast. Patrick. He weaseled his way into the family and moved back to Alberta with her before they were married. She had faith in him. He transferred credits to the U of L before dropping out of drama after a couple years. Always told the family it was because of "professional differences" with one of the directors. So he went to work for an oil company, then worked as a librarian, then as a city worker, then for the municipal pound where he got the mastiff. Betty stayed married through a couple of kids, Gloria and Brady, until figuring out that her husband was emotionally unstable and had a temper short as a matchstick. I won't say all that he's done, but it has been plenty. Now Betty's gone to Edmonton with the kids and Patrick's stuck with the house playing penny songs on the piano, old show tunes from high school, to try and drum up some pathos.

And he drives around during the day fixing potholes and picking up strays and cleaning the pound.

In short, everyone around here thinks he's a fairly pathetic human being.

At Costco, I was looking at computers when I ran into a fellow schoolteacher, Dirk Hancock. We'd been talking about the Cosmos, the local high school basketball team, contenders for the provincial championship title. They were slated to play LCI at zones in a week and Dirk was complaining that he couldn't go. Wife had to be at the playhouse for their production for *Big River*. It was the dress rehearsal and she wanted him home with the kids. "I'll just take them to provincials anyway," he said. But I knew better. Three kids under five at home and my bet's on the husband to do what she says. Plus, I couldn't see Dirk lugging around two toddlers at the Sportsplex. Just not his style. Then he got on this tirade about the playhouse and it taking up too much time. "Isn't your old brother-in-law one of the head honchos for that thing?" he asked me.

"Yeah," I said. Didn't want to e-la-bo-rate.

"Doesn't he know it's provincials?"

The way Dirk said it, it sounded like everyone knew about provincials, like if you were born and raised in southern Alberta, you would know. You wouldn't require *anyone* to go to some dress rehearsal when a bunch of teenage boys were playing their hearts out on the big court at the Sportsplex. I just shrugged. "We have to dog-sit for him."

"No shit," Dirk said.

I could tell Dirk thought that was pretty funny. Me, the assistant coach to the Cosmos, dog-sitting Patrick's behemoth during provincials while he emotes in blackface, laying it on thick as the only authentic southern drawl in town.

"Audrey's taking care of him," I said.

That night, I asked Audrey if she'd dog-sit for Pat.

"I thought you told him we couldn't."

"It's the last time," I said. "Kennel was full. He said to just check on him. Make sure he's OK."

"Why doesn't he just leave him out on Halpern's farm?"

"Would you leave him anywhere with other animals?"

Audrey sat back in her chair. It was time for pre-pillow pillow talk. Always get everything out of the way. Never stay angry. Communication. Audrey's always been a well-ordered person.

"Parsons just got the new fence up," she said. The Parsons were our other neighbors. Like having a fence made dog-sitting just as much their responsibility.

"They have a rat terrier."

"You let people walk all over you, you know."

"This isn't about me," I said.

Audrey sighed. "I know," she said.

Practice was about the only place I felt sane anymore. On the court, directing the guys. In a game or running drills, everything made sense. I'm the playbook maker, responsible for our offensive attack. That year we had talent and room for improvement. With help, I knew that we could make it to provincials, maybe even win. Brennan and Myers were good. As a center, Brennan had height and he could post up just about anyone. And "Mongoose" Myers, our quick point guard, had arms and legs like pistons firing all the time. And control. And a more-than-decent 3-point shot if he couldn't work it inside.

Dan Myers, the head coach, was Mongoose's dad. Our last game, the boys had trouble with defense, so we set the gym up with stations. One kid had the ball and another kid guarded him, trying to get the ball away. They went up the gym floor and back. Once they were finished, they ran sprints and did push-ups on the baseline, the forty-five, and then the center all across the gym. After that, they were dog-tired during Dan's speech.

Dan talked plays. The worry this weekend, he said, was the big guy, Mark Kyler, number 48, LCI's center. Dan didn't want him messing up our inside game, so he was putting a lot of pressure on Brennan to make good decisions in the paint and kick it back out to Mongoose if he didn't have a shot. "If you do go up," Dan said, "face him and go straight up with it. Try and get him off his feet, then come pushing up from underneath the guy to draw the foul." OK, I thought. I could live with that. But then he introduced play five. We always reserved five for special circumstances. Usually it was a variation on our pick and roll with one of the forwards and the center crossing through the key to create a lane for the other forward, or it was an attempt at feeding the ball to Mongoose. I didn't have a problem with either of those plays. Another assistant might worry about favoritism, but even though Mongoose was Dan's son, he was still the best damn point guard in the league and we knew it.

"I want you throwing elbows," Dan said. "Anything you can if that boy starts crowding you."

I cleared my throat.

"Then if Mongoose runs five, I want all of you to stick to your man. I don't care if you have to step on their feet. Try to make it subtle, though. Pull on their jerseys or nudge them a certain way. And then feed the ball back to Mongoose as soon as he's open. Don't play dirty, play smart."

I don't know what I expected. Hoosier goodness or something, but this was not my style at all and the boys seemed to be lapping it up like wildcats. Dirty was *exactly* how Dan was telling them to play.

I interrupted him. "Could I talk to you for a second, Dan?" Silence. All the joking stopped. Dan followed me to the end of the room.

"I have a problem with the play," I said.

"What about it."

"It stinks."

Dan laughed. "You're just sore's all."

"No I'm not. You want the kids to respect you. They won't if you're telling them to take cheap shots."

He looked amazed. "We need every competitive advantage, Gale."

"I don't like it," I said.

"No one asked you to."

Dan was right. I was sore, sore that he had gone over my head like that, just jumped into the play without even talking to me beforehand. And the play did stink, elbows, pulling jerseys, "drawing" fouls. Dan sometimes took things to the extreme. Like the first week of practice where the boys couldn't go home until they puked from the exercise. He never said it outright, but they knew. We all knew.

At home Audrey was doing Pilates. She scissored through the air and gasped, breathing in numbers like she was sucking on an inhaler. She stopped, stretched, and held her legs so they touched the ground over her head.

"These would do wonders for your abs," she said.

Wonders. Gale Warden. Eighth Freaking wonder of the world.

"They make me fart," I said.

"You're disgusting."

I didn't argue, but went to go out with our dog, Zeke. I gave him a warped square of rawhide and he pawed the glass on the rear patio door to go and bury it. Zeke came back with dirt on his nose. "Where's your treat?" I asked him. He looked at me. "Go get it," I said.

I didn't really expect him to, but he pawed at the door again and I let him out. I followed him to the garden, Audrey's row of bulbs. Mole-sized dirt mounds packed down, waiting for warmer spring weather. He dug away at the end, brought me his rawhide with an expression like "What's next?"

"I wish I knew," I said. He put the rawhide in my hand and I wiped the dirt and dog slobber off on my jeans. On the other side of the fence, I could barely make out Patrick through the slats. He was kneeling in the middle of the yard with Otis.

"Say a prayer for the Cosmos," I said.

Patrick got up. "You can't stop Mother Nature," he said. He had a trowel in his hand, terry cloth gardening gloves. "You should've seen it, Gale. Otis just jumped up and caught it–bam!–mid-swoop."

"What did he catch?"

"A robin. A big, fat one."

"A round robin?"

"Just buried it. You ever seen anything like that?"

No, I thought, I hadn't. Only dog we ever had was Zeke and he was big enough, but not athletic. Never even chased gophers when we took him out to the ridge. Part of me kind of hoped he would. Otis, on the other hand, was a real champ. Had about every hunting instinct known to dogs and he wasn't shy about showing it. He was kind of like Patrick, in a way. You know that old saying how an owner resembles his dog? Patrick was a showman, but only when other people were around. I knew. Being a neighbor, you see the days he sat just watching that 10-inch set on his patio. Working for the town was less than a part-time job. It was being in front of people that set Pat off. That's why, when they started up the town playhouse, he was the first in line. Give him a costume and an audience and the guy'll do anything.

"So the Cosmos have a big game this weekend, eh?"

"Yeah. I've been meaning to talk to you about that."

"About the game?"

"No, about your practice. Your dress rehearsal. There's a few people who've complained about it being at the same time as provincials."

"We only have five days until opening night."

"You could still move it back a day. Dirk Hancock says there's no reason you couldn't do it Saturday."

"We have practice then, too," Pat said.

"Oh."

"These things take time."

"Guess so."

I said goodbye to Patrick and went back inside after Zeke took a crap on our lawn.

In school the next day I graded a test in Math 30. Some of the other teachers think I'm a pussy for taking class time like I do, but I always tell them that I'll start taking work home when they start paying me. The government's tighter than a banker's ass. With math you can get away with it. Grading usually doesn't take the whole class anyway. It's not like essays or short answer questions. There's only one right answer. Then afterwards I'll look them over again, maybe give part marks for questions where students did most of the work, but messed up on the calculation. It's only fair.

At the end of class, I sat down to go through the tests and enter the marks into my grade book. I had a spare the next period. Not many students did well on this test. We were just starting to get into minor calculus, and the class didn't get it, Mongoose Myers in particular. Most of the test was blank and I had to give him a failing grade. That wasn't much of a problem in itself–I often have students bomb a couple of tests–but his overall performance in the class had been borderline, barely passing. Since we'd only had two major tests so far, this put him well below the benchmark for competing in school sports. I flipped through the test again and gave him points for any partially completed equations, but with the blank questions I couldn't do much of anything. His score was dismally low, and I was more aware than anyone how much we needed him for provincials this next weekend, especially against powerhouse LCI. I resolved to talk with Dan that evening about it.

Practice went at a relentless pace. We decided we'd work hard until Wednesday, getting the boys ready. Then we'd back off on Thursday, act like we were going to drill them just as hard, but then let them leave after shooting a couple hoops. "Great work, boys" we'd tell them, hoping that the morale would carry over into the game. I loved little psychological tricks like that. During the practice, we ran play five with our starters up against the second string. The second stringers were taking a beating. They'd be boxed out, jabbed, and held just to clear a lane for Mongoose to snake through to the basket. One big kid—a Coppins—went down and his knee skinned the floor, squeaking like new rubber. The play didn't stop, just slowed for a moment, the kids watching Dan to see how they should react. "Stop like that in a game and I'll bust your ass," he yelled. "How do you think the refs know to call a foul?" I watched from the sidelines, arms folded. This wasn't the time to bother Dan, but I felt that I had something over him on principles. If I talked to him now, maybe he'd stop these kids from beating the hell out of each other. Sure enough, when I called him over, he broke up the play, sent the kids around the gym for laps and then to the showers.

"It's Mongoose," I told him. "He's failing my class."

"What about it?"

"Foreman won't put up with it," I said, half sure.

"Leave Foreman to me. He's a prick anyway, Gale. He'd let him play if we put the pressure on. All you're going to do is make a stink for nothing."

"Probably," I said.

"Controversy for controversy's sake."

I thought about that for a moment. We'd had our share of controversy the last couple years—the two super seniors we took from Milk River in '92 and then the effigy of a Brazilian exchange student that our players beat with a baseball bat at a pep rally. Letting a flunking student play would certainly get some headlines. "I don't know, Dan. This whole thing—the five play, letting Mongoose slide for the game—just what exactly is he learning here? I mean his

test was blank, Dan. Blank. Like he wanted to prove that
he didn't pass. Aren't you concerned about his character?"

"When you start having kids, maybe I'll let you talk to
me about raising mine."

"Dan . . ."

"I'll see you tomorrow."

At home, Otis was wrestling with Zeke.

"I thought you didn't want him over," I said.

"Zeke was bored," Audrey said. "He was climbing over
everything when I got home."

The two dogs ran at each other, jumping in the air,
their rib cages colliding. They used their forelegs like giant
tongs to grasp each other, to try to get on top.

"What about his neck?"

"I put bitter apple spray on it."

The dogs stopped for a second, exhausted. Otis
snapped his teeth, just missing Zeke's head. He licked
Zeke's neck. Then snapped again.

"Not bad," I said.

"That's what I thought."

We both stood and watched out the screen door. Zeke
still would try to fit his mouth around Otis' neck, but Otis
wasn't returning the favor. He just bit into the air, then
licked Zeke's coat. Otis barked.

Audrey left to change for Pilates and I flicked on the
TV to get some news before she claimed it for her work-
out. It was local coverage of an airplane accident–small
craft–that flew into the hoodoos at Writing-on-Stone. The
pilot was a woman–a Hutterite originally from Wolf Creek
colony. Her family refused to be interviewed.

"Mongoose failed his math test today," I said.

Audrey stretched on the floor, lying with her stomach
down, her arms reaching for her feet. "Too bad," she said.

"Myers wants me to ignore it."

"What does Foreman say?" She moved onto her side
and brought her right leg up perpendicular to her body.

"He doesn't know yet. But he'd probably let him play."

"Probably?"

"Probably."

Audrey switched sides and extended her other leg upwards. I had seen this routine so many times before that I had the steps already worked out in my mind. Next she would sit, then do leg lifts, then scissors. Then the exercises for her abs.

"You should really talk to him, though."

"Who?

"Foreman. He's the one who decides."

"Myers is worried about making a stink."

"It's his son causing the problem."

"That's what I told him. Then he gave me a lecture about not having children."

"He didn't."

"Did."

"And what did you say?"

"I told him I'd see him tomorrow."

"That really isn't fair."

"I know."

Audrey turned the TV off and sat up. "He knows we can't have kids."

"I know," I said.

Audrey stomped off down the hallway. She cursed over her shoulder. "Sometimes I wonder why we don't move to a normal town."

I decided to go get some videos of pre-Jordan games from Reg, the guy who ran Jimmy's, the only convenience store in town. I wanted to see Kareem and Magic Johnson in their prime, squeaking around in their Converse. Reg had years of them he'd collected and ordered special for sports junkies, and I went regularly, sometimes watching games over and over again, not only for the spectacular end-of-the-game shots or close championship games, but for the plays. I felt that I could, at times, look into some of those great players' minds, see the court mapped out like a grid with players moving to their spots, drawing out the defense and getting the ball inside. It wasn't far to the other end of town, but it was night, and in Ridgeview you see your students everywhere, and that was enough to keep me in my car. Outside of my context as a coach or teacher, I always felt awkward, like I should be telling the kids that they needed to be somewhere or work harder. In your car, you could just lift a finger to wave.

When I passed the playhouse, I noticed Dirk Hancock banging on one of the front doors. I slowed down. Then he walked to the side door and banged on that. His mouth moved and he dented the toe kick with his boot. I rolled down my window.

"What's the trouble?"

"My kids not knowing their mother's the trouble," he said. He banged on the door again, walked back to the front double doors.

I parked next to his minivan and noticed his two toddlers strapped inside, terrified. Dirk strutted up the walk like a speed walker and was banging and yelling again, and I went after him. Just as I passed the side door, Pat poked his head out.

"Gale?" he asked.

"Not me, him." I pointed.

Pat pushed the door open and wedged a piece of wood underneath to keep it there, then walked out to where I was standing. "Is my wife in there?" Dirk yelled when he saw us.

"Calm down, Dirk," Pat said. The front door opened and Dirk went inside. "You'd better be here for this." Pat motioned me to follow him.

We were right next to the stage where most of the cast stood arranged in a chorus. We skirted the band pit and came out in front when Dirk entered from the back and strutted up the middle aisle. His wife, Loralee, plucked herself from between two hefty sopranos and made her way down to meet him.

"Let's take the Coda one more time, beat by beat, and see if we can't get the descant right this time, shall we?" Pat gestured for the band to start playing and the chorus sang, "I'm waiting for the light to shine" with a soprano up high trying to give it southern gospel grace. I kept to the side and watched the confrontation, Loralee waving her hands, shaking her head, Dirk folding his arms and finally sitting down. He pointed to the chair. Loralee walked curtly back to the stage, and gathered her things, then waited to talk to Pat at the end of the song. Pat motioned me over and Dirk watched with his arms folded across his chest and his back straight up in the chair.

"Her husband wants her to leave now," Pat explained. "He's throwing a fit."

"Looks calm enough to me."

"Couldn't you explain to him—you're good at this, Gale—couldn't you explain that we need Loralee in the play. She has a major role."

"It's not *that* major," Loralee said. "You could get by with Geraldine on alto."

"We need you in the second act," Pat said. "You're Alice's daughter."

"I only have a few lines. Geraldine could learn it."

Pat shook his head. "Really I don't know what to do. That man comes in here and just expects you to leave. Couldn't you talk to him, Gale? Explain things to him?"

"I want no part of this."

"Just talk to him."

"This is a domestic affair." I felt like I was some kid on the playground relaying messages back and forth between lovers, unable to face each other. I left and sat down next to Dirk in the audience. To his credit, Pat kept the troupe occupied so that they weren't caught gawking at the angry Dirk who was ready to shut the whole thing down.

"You're such a pussy, Gale," he said.

"Whatever you said sure scared her. She's ready to leave."

Dirk laughed. "I just told her what the kids tell me."

"Is it really that big of a deal?"

Dirk said. "I'm not leaving until she does."

"Suit yourself." I shrugged my shoulders to Patrick. Pat whispered something to Loralee and she took her bags and walked toward us. When she neared Dirk, they didn't touch. But by the way Dirk followed her out of the building, he might as well have been holding her forcefully by the elbow, ushering her out the door like a criminal.

I talked to Mongoose the next day, pulled him aside at the end of class and waited for everyone else to file through the door so that we were alone.

"I'm going to have to report your progress in my class, Mongoose. Which means that you probably won't be able to play this weekend."

"It's zones . . ."

"No one knows that better than me," I said. "But I still feel that we need to stop this now. You might not get to play this weekend, but you're limiting your progress in other ways."

"Dad's not going to like this."

"I've already talked to your father."

"I could retake the test," Mongoose said. "I'll do better this time." Mongoose produced his largely blank test and handed it to me. I flipped through it, surprised at how generous I had been with the few areas where he had made some effort.

"The test is almost blank," I said. "You can drop one test at the end of the semester. Maybe that will make a difference. But right now you're failing my class."

"The test is blank because you said that we shouldn't guess."

"That's for multiple choice exams."

"How was I supposed to know that? You always say it's better not to guess."

I had always been precise and clear when I talked about my grading; though quarter-right-minus-wrong was a hard concept for some to understand, everyone knew that it only applied to multiple-choice examinations. Perhaps it was my own desire to win against LCI that Friday or Mongoose's apparent sincerity, but I found myself thinking, *could be, you know.* It was the first time that I had had Mongoose in any of my classes, so I surprised myself when I said, "I'll talk with principal Foreman about it," realizing, as I did so, that I had no intention of talking to Foreman or anyone else for that matter. Mongoose was going to play.

Audrey says I use too many sports metaphors when I talk about life and she's probably right. But there is something about the shape of a basketball in your hand, the pressure from its weight as you cradle it in your palm with your arm cocked at 90 degrees that makes you want to tell the world. It's like basketball, pure and simple. You aim, you've got your potential energy, you release. If it's on target, you're a winner. The way my life was going, I felt like a guard forced to play center in a game with no rules. I was getting tromped, walloped, beaten, and there wasn't anything I could do to prevent it. Audrey saw me moping and tried to settle me down. "Think of Saturday," she said. "It'll all be over then." She thought that I was fretting about the game, but it was more than that. It was waking up in the morning and feeling like a shit. The purpose of my profession was slipping away from me. The meager rewards of teaching were so ephemeral, so delayed. For every student saying "Yo, teach, thanks," there were fifty others wishing you'd never been born. It was enough to make me consider a career change more than once. I had always wanted to build something; I fancied starting my own business, or going into real estate, something that had immediate impact on people's lives, where I could chalk up successes like, well, baskets.

"Coach Warden and I have been pleased with the work you guys have been doing these past few weeks," Dan said. I anticipated the end of Dan's speech where all the players would yell enthusiastically and Dan would have them shoot a couple hoops, then dress down and relax for tomorrow.

"Coach, is it true that Mongoose isn't going to play?"

"No, that's not true." Dan didn't even blink. The conversation was over before most guys even knew what was being said. But that didn't stop the impact it had. When Dan let them loose, they were almost cautious in their excitement, as though we or the school or the county might hold some trump card that we were itching to play, to punish them for their good fortune, their efforts in making this year's team the best it could be.

At the game, Foreman was dressed in black and white, the Cosmos' colors. Big black deal with white sleeves, a letterman's jacket from his own glory days over thirty years ago. Foreman had sausage-sized fingers and walked with a cane. The Sportsplex was full; even though it wasn't in our hometown, a whole side of the building was swathed in our school colors.

"Look at all the rooters," I said.

He laughed. "Let's just hope we give them something to root for!"

It was a joke between us: rooters/root. Ever since the doe-eyed exchange student from Australia came to Ridgeview two years ago and she told us that it meant "hookers" back home. Every game we had a whole lot of them. Hookers everywhere.

"Mongoose playing tonight?"

"Sure," I said.

"Good," he said. "Dan told me you had some trouble?"

"Just getting borderline marks," I said. "He could use some outside tutoring."

"That boy will go a long way," Foreman said.

"I sure hope so."

Foreman and I shook hands. I went onto the floor. The boys had just dressed down and were coming out in their warm-up suits. They took shots until we organized them into two lines for doing lay-ups. Brennan dunked every so often, another psychological trick. Keep dunking and the other team notices, the fans notice. People get pumped up. The Sportsplex speakers boomed, "Unbelievable." Fucking unbelievable.

We had our starters and the refs came over and introduced themselves. They made us check the boys for jewelry and watches, told us to play clean, a real best-man-wins pep talk. The boys had been fed plenty of that. Me, with my moral, you-reap-what-you-sow advice and Dan with his "Let's clobber them" speech that I'd heard him give so many times. As usual, he waited until just before the game started, the boys all the time thinking, this is it, this is the big one. Then Dan just stood there and said, "Let's clobber them," grinning on one side of his face like they were sharing a secret. The game's all about secrets. All of it.

We sang "O Canada" and took our seats. Brennan set up against LCI's center, tipped the ball away back to Mongoose. He had height but Kyler, #48, was a bruiser. Big ham-sized legs and shoulders he used all the time to box out under the glass. I found myself thinking like Dan. With the right finesse, Brennan could draw the foul, even make dirt look clean.

We took an early lead. Mongoose executed plays easily, like a traffic cop out in the middle of rush hour. He pulled the ball out, brought it back to the top of the key when they couldn't work an inside shot. The plays flowed seamlessly, with our pick-and-roll game shredding LCI's defense. We ended the first quarter with a 12-point lead and our players in good spirits. At times like this, Dan's advice was best: just ride the wave. Clobber them. I'd seen Dan relish a double-digit pounding even in exhibition games against 1A schools like Stirling or Warner. Never let up, he always said. Never get in the way of a good thing.

Near the end of the half we lost some of our lead. Logan Frye took a personal foul that sent LCI's point guard to the line. The boys' initial euphoria was dying down, and Kyler started using his weight against Brennan. And there were three turnovers on bad passes picked off by one of LCI's forwards. At halftime they had whittled down the lead to two points and I knew that we were licked.

You'd think that as assistant coach I needed to be more optimistic. I'd seen enough games to know that anything could happen in high school sports. Teams could come from behind with a 30-point deficit to win. The starters could get benched in the second half on personal fouls. You just never knew. But I had this theory about energy that I generally kept to myself. I had tested it in my own way, observed the players, listened to the onset of foul language, oaths and trash-talking, and Dan's incessant drilling from the sidelines. Dan didn't know it, but so much of my theory came from him. Not his "advice" or no-holds-barred attitude, but his general comportment with the players. When we started off strong, like we had tonight, it generated an energy that Dan couldn't see. Then if we lost our lead, he went berserk. Dan looked for blame in the players and targeted their weaknesses. He pushed the team captains harder. He yelled. The negativity grew until the team was blocked. They missed shots, they stumbled, all until the last whistle blew and we were out of the game.

At half time, Dan rushed to the dressing room with me tagging behind.

"What is this?" Dan asked, holding out a basketball in his hand.

The players looked incredulous. One of those answers that was so obvious that no one wanted to speak, even though everyone was thinking over and over again, "Basketball, basketball, basketball."

"Hmmm?" Dan asked.

"It's a basketball, Coach," Mongoose said.

"That's right," Dan said. "It's a basketball."

I phoned Audrey on my cell after Dan's inspirational speech. Control the basketball, he said. A simple task. It's small, round, solid. But it's much more. Control the basketball and you are master of the game. The game could mean seasons; it could mean provincials, talent scouts. Everything came spiraling out from this simple brown leather ball. Control the basketball and you control the world.

"I'll never use another sports metaphor as long as I live," I said when she picked up the phone.

"Gale?" she said. "Aren't you in the middle of the game?"

"Halftime. How are the dogs?"

"Fine," she said.

I felt suddenly stupid there, holding the phone. I told Audrey that I'd see her in a couple of hours; then I bumped into Dirk Hancock on my way to the floor. "Enjoying the game?" I asked. He just smiled and raised a paper Coke cup to me. "That's right," he said, no kids in sight. I wanted to stop and chat, but Dan was waving me down. We only had a couple minutes of half-time left.

The buzzer sounded and our starters cleared the bench. The second half began like the first. We were, seemingly, in control. Mongoose ran the plays like clockwork, and we kept the game crisp and neat. He passed it inside and only drove for the basket when he saw a clear lane. Smart plays. But it wouldn't last. LCI called a time-out and came back doing a full-court press that our boys weren't prepared for. LCI stuck to their players and Mongoose was caught on an over and back for a change of possession. Our passes got weak. Dan yelled like hell. Brennan in particular was having problems. His strength was waning. Jockeying for position under the boards against the Kyler behemoth was getting to him. He was losing agility on offence and his defense was going fast. The other players were faring equally poorly and Frye was in foul trouble. Dan called time-out. We were down four points.

"Frye, you're out for the game. Taylor, you're in. I want you to help out on Kyler when you can. Do anything you can to keep him from going up under the basket. Start running five if the lead gets to six points. Their guards are tired, so push them hard." No criticism this time, just direction. Dan wanted to win the game.

The guys hit the court enraged. Taylor was a big kid, energetic, a follower. He kept in close and used the players' bodies to screen his shoves. The kid was a magician. Only an expert would be able to see the inside nudges or see how his trash talk affected Kyler and the other players. Dan's wild card seemed to be working. Then it happened. Kyler took a pass and was about to drive in. Taylor was in the lane at the bottom of the key. Kyler came off his pivot foot and around a pick, right into Taylor, who grabbed at Kyler's jersey as he sprawled backwards. Kyler lost his balance and fell over. The ref called *charging* and the LCI coach yelled, "Are you blind?" Taylor went to the line and sunk both baskets. Kyler was pissed.

The play kept heating up when my phone started buzzing in my coat pocket. I chose to ignore it. We had two minutes left and we were still down a basket. Kyler had three personals now, but it was near the end of the game and LCI couldn't afford to take him out. Then Mongoose made a great play on the full-court press, snatching it away on a weak throw-in and driving for the basket. We were tied. LCI came up the court quickly, then passed it to Kyler who was on the baseline. Brennan was on him and pulled his jersey when he went up. He missed the shot. No call and the Cosmos didn't wait for one. Kyler yelled at the ref as he trotted back down the court, but by then Brennan had already scored and we were up a basket. We were winning with less than a minute left. Then something unexpected happened. LCI worked their way up to the top of the key and got it inside again to Kyler. Big mistake. Taylor and Brennan came at him from both sides as he tried to power his way through. He took cheap shots from both of them on the way in, missed the basket and Brennan fell backwards, drawing the foul. Kyler came down with the ball and slammed it to the floor so hard that it bounced twenty feet in the air. Then he shoved Taylor who just shrugged. A fan threw a plastic cup filled with ice water on the court. Three LCI guys came off the bench and Kyler tried to shake a referee who had him in a bear hug. Whistles were blowing everywhere.

It took all the refs, coaches, and several policemen to calm the place down. Both benches had entered into the fray and several parents were throwing punches. It was a mess. The refs met together and decided on a personal foul for Kyler and a technical for the team. Kyler was out of the game and LCI was deflated. All we had to do afterwards was clean up.

Dan was laughing. "That'll teach him to lose his temper," he said.

Taylor sunk the first two baskets and we were up by three. He bricked the last one and Mongoose got the rebound for another basket. We eased off the full-court press and the guys were already celebrating. They had reason to. We were, after all, going to provincials. My phone was buzzing against my side again and I couldn't ignore it any longer. Someone was trying to get a hold of me. I'm a sucker for that; every time at home, I'm the one getting the phone. Audrey just sits there, reading her book or doing her Pilates and lets it ring. I wasn't surprised when it was her on the line.

"It's Zeke," she said when I asked what was wrong.

"What happened?" I could hear the muffled voice of someone talking in the background—a man—repeating his apologies over and over again.

"We're taking him to the vet," she said. "Pat thinks his neck might be broken. He's still alive."

I heard the buzzer go. Our guys were off the bench, running to the center of the court, arms raised. The scoreboard had us up by seven points: 88-81. The Sportsplex erupted in cheers. I bent over, cupping my hand around the phone to hear more closely. I pushed my way off the court and out to one of the concrete entrances, big enough for a Zamboni to get through. I heard a man's voice on the line. It was Pat.

"I don't know how it could've happened," he said. "It's not like Otis at all." His voice was cornstalk dry.

"I'll meet you there," I said and hung up.

Leaving wasn't as hard as I thought it would be. I caught everyone off guard while they were celebrating. I was sick of the game, the bad calls, Dan's intimidation tactics, the Cosmos, the whole damn town. I thought of leaning over to Dan and saying, "I quit" about a thousand times, with vengeance. But instead I slipped out, like a thief, or a con artist off on a swindle. I raced to my car and sped the whole way to our vet's. I imagined Zeke's head, bitten by Otis, bloodied and battered. I thought of those cartoons where Bugs Bunny is in Elmer Fudd's hunting breeches. They're filled with water and Fudd shoots them, riddling them with holes. The water comes out, streaming like a fountain. I thought of Zeke spurting blood that way, from his chest, his neck, his groin. I turned on the radio, which I rarely do, to give the air around me space, to fill up the empty car, give my anger something to gnaw on. When I reached the turnoff to Welling, I noticed an RCMP patrol car. It pulled me to the side of the road, its lights flashing like Christmas in my rear-view mirror. I pulled over.

"Do you know how fast you were going?"

Do I know? Of course I do, I thought. I broke the law. I was speeding.

"I'm not sure. I wasn't paying attention."

The cop chewed me out, gave me a ticket despite my contrition. I wanted the cop to yank me out of the vehicle,

cuff my hands behind my back and read me my rights like
they do in the movies. I watched the car in my mirror. The
cop had turned on the interior lights and he had his head
down, like he was praying, filling out my inevitable ticket.
I wanted to explain to him why I was upset and speeding
during the LCI/Cosmos game when everyone I knew was
either in the Sportsplex, or dressed in southern rags and
pantomiming in blackface. I pushed open my door and
put both legs out onto the concrete. He would understand,
wouldn't he? Let me explain?

"Get back in the car, please."

The cop had a megaphone. Or something. I couldn't
tell where the sound came from, but there it was, like God,
shaking his finger. I pulled my legs back in, and waited for
my ticket, for the police officer to tap on my window with
his stick, then hand the carbon copy to me and explain the
reason for the fine. It would happen, I knew. It would happen because it had to. But damn it, I thought. Really. He
had no right.

TORCHED

I met Jeb my first day on the roofing crew for Charlton and Hill. That summer, we re-roofed the Ridgeview swimming pool. I started on a manual tear-off machine, a cast-iron deal that looked like a giant pitching wedge with handles that I used to pry up layers of old tar, particle board, and yellow insulation. Dennis, our foreman, said we were putting on a torch roof, though neither Jeb nor I, both first year grunts on the job, had ever laid one. I jammed the tear-off machine under the roof and Jeb picked up the broken layers and threw them into a dumpster.

"You're more likely to get injured as a roofer than if you were a cop," Jeb said.

"At least you can get worker's comp," I said. "The high life. Gary said last summer one kid smashed his thumb and got three weeks paid vacation."

The machine didn't seem to be working right. In the morning before break I had tried to remove just the top layer of tar and gravel. Jeb held it while I slid the machine underneath, tearing off the top layer in a long roll that would break when it got too heavy. Then Dennis told us to hurry up, that we looked like a couple of dainty bitches doing our nails. We pushed along the top layer for a while longer, aiming to tear the tar off faster, but then Dennis came over, flung me aside, grabbed the machine, and drove it underneath all the layers: particle board, tar, insulation, the whole bit. He heaved down like he was doing dips for his lats, and forced the roof up in chunks that we scrambled to grab. I tried doing tear-off like Dennis with mild success. Pushing under all those layers took too much power for the long haul and the whole process was messy; insulation splintered all over the place. By the afternoon we were peeling off the top layer again in long strips. Quick and clean.

At break, Jeb kept complaining. None of us wanted to hear it. There were four grunts on the crew: a high school dropout doing temp work; Gary, who went to Lethbridge Community College and worked at Charlton and Hill over the summer to pay off gambling debts; and Jeb and me, the two university kids trying to raise money for tuition in the fall. Charlton and Hill recycled our kind like old newspaper. Other grunts had stories of guys showing up for work in sweats and a t-shirt and having to go home after ten minutes of shoveling gravel or doing tear off.

"If we go by statistics, one of us is going to get it by the end of the summer," Jeb said.

"I hope it's me," I said.

"You guys are both crazy," Gary said. "No one is going to fucking 'get it.' I mean, who the fuck cares?"

"I care. Do you know how many people have already died in my graduating class? Four. Four guys all my age and I'm working on a roofing crew," Jeb said.

The high school kid, Brent, was stretched out on the grass, shaded by the swimming pool roof. He pushed himself up on his elbows.

"If you're so worried, why don't you quit?" Brent asked.

"That's what you would like, right? Just get me to quit and everyone will have a party."

"You're a moron," Gary said.

The next day, it was windy. Wind can be disastrous during tear off. Jeb found this out while he was holding up a sheet of yellow insulation the size of a door. He lifted it up sideways into the wind, and when he turned, the board caught like a sail and it pulled Jeb to the edge of the roof. Dennis yelled, "Let go," and the insulation flew off the roof and into the empty concrete pool. Dennis came over and said, "What are you, stupid?" and told Jeb to get his ass down there and clean up. We kept tearing off, trying to keep the heavier pieces of gravel and tar on top so that the insulation and particle board didn't fly out past the dumpster and into the gravel alley that flanked the pool.

"Next summer I'm working for my uncle. A nice desk job. Something where I don't have to worry about getting blown away," Jeb said when he came back.

"It was your own fucking fault," Gary said. "Get over it."

"A hazardous work environment. My uncle would never stand for this kind of treatment either—like Dennis, Mr. Cro-Magnon man. You know the intern my uncle had last year pulled in six figures and that was just a summer job."

"Bullshit," Gary said. "No one makes that kind of money."

"Investment bankers do. It all depends on what kind of work you do for him. If you're pulling in six figures, you're doing him a favor. The more money you make, the more money he makes."

Gary looked like he was ready to throw Jeb off the roof.

"Just about lunch," I said—the only thing anyone said until Dennis called break. Then we got out of the heat on the roof and settled down next to the pool.

I pitched myself on the ground, opened up my thermos and guzzled my four liters of Gatorade. Brent was already out, napping I think, and Gary ran across the street to get something from Jimmy's, the local convenience store. It was Jeb and me. "So what's an investment banker do?" I asked. I'd be damned if I didn't find out about his uncle, even if Gary thought it was a pile of horse shit.

"You invest money for clients. The reason you can make a shitload of money is because of the commission. You make them money, they make you money."

"Not a bad deal," I said. A van drove up and parked not far from us and two men got out and walked into the pool building. "Hey, maybe they're filling the pool."

"About time." It was Brent, talking through his hat. He had it over his face, brim covering his neck. "Could use a swim."

"So what about this job," I said. "You think he'll let you work for him next year?"

Jeb picked through his lunch, fingered a bag of carrot sticks. "Depends," he said. "This year he said that the company was worried about nepotism and they didn't think that I was old enough for the internship. You have to be either graduated or graduating the following year. But I think he'd do it if he thought that I was qualified. Work for him, though, and you'd be making bank. And you wouldn't have to be anyone's slave."

Gary came back with three pops and a sandwich. He carried all three pops with one hand, holding them by the necks. "Won two fucking freebies," he said.

On Monday we started doing torch roof. Took a truck full of PVC roof cap and brought it along with a tar kettle and a couple pallets of particle board, tar paper, mops, and blue foamy insulation. We worked the roof in layers. Brent and I laid the tar paper while Dennis fired up the kettle, then showed us how to nail. You let the nail dangle between your index and middle finger, then you pounded it in. Dennis nailed with one stroke, moving up and down the rows of tar paper like a machine. The rest of us started out with two or three hits each, and we sometimes missed. But the hammer didn't hurt our hands, not if we held the nails right and trusted our aim. Then we started with the tar, called "hot." Jeb got stuck with it. He was almost always behind. Dennis would yell, "Hot," and we'd look over to see Jeb struggling with a black bucket of tar that he'd filled using the spout that led up from the kettle to the roof. Dennis would swear again and then Jeb would be running.

If Jeb was late, Dennis held up the mop to show how it was already stiff. Dennis wouldn't let anyone else touch the mop. There was technique to it, I guess. Swirling it in the right number or arcs. Making sure it was always moving. Dennis orchestrated when and where we should put the sheets of particle board and got upset when we slid sheets into each other, sending a lip of tar up through the cracks. It was slow moving, but by lunch time, we had half the roof mopped and covered with particle board. Brent and I climbed down with Gary and met Jeb and Derek in the shade. Jeb was covered with bits of tar, had slashes of it on his jeans and his gloves, and licorice-colored stains on his shirt.

Jeb unrolled his sleeve, showed me his arm. "Damn hot burns right through the fabric," he said. There was a wedge-shaped spot of pink on his arm the size of a penny. "Dennis has got me on hot on purpose." He shook his arm out until the sleeve hung over his hand.

"You're a fucking pansy," Gary said.

That shut Jeb up quick. We ate in silence. Brent wolfed down his food and then started his ritual nap. Jeb scraped pieces of tar off his jeans, winced like he was picking scabs that hadn't quite healed underneath.

"I have a friend who died last year working a summer job," Jeb said. Gary didn't look our way, but I could tell that he was paying attention, probably bristling with every word.

"Doing what?" I said.

"Oil rigs in northern Alberta. You know those great big trucks they use to deforest? He was driving one of those down a hill and the brakes went out. I heard that he tried to drive it off into the trees but he lost control and crashed. I went to the funeral, you know. Closed coffin service."

"Will someone fucking shut him up?" Gary said.

"Another friend—his name was Jerry—he died roofing shingles. But it was from an accident he had when he was in high school. He was riding his bike at midnight out in the country and there weren't any lights so he couldn't see very well. A woman–an older woman–was riding the opposite direction and they *hit heads.* Can you believe that? Smacked right into her. They had him in the hospital for a subdural hemorrhage. He was fine for a couple years, but then one summer he was roofing his house with his dad, got a headache and went inside to sleep it off. He never woke up."

"Why are you even telling us this?" Gary said. "So your friends died working summer jobs, so what?"

"No reason. Just thought it was interesting."

Gary ignored Jeb all afternoon when we started on the thicker insulation. I laid the sheets down and Jeb screwed them in. Then Brent and Gary rolled out the PVC roof and Dennis ran the torch, lifting up the overlap and melting the inside before pressing it down with the back of a metal hook. The torch fascinated me. Dennis moved with such precision, holding the overlap open with the hook and the side of his boot. I asked him about doing torch when it was break and he said that I could with a little training, and before I knew it, I had the job. The next couple days, I melted the rubber off the end of my steel-toed boots to the metal shank from torching.

About that time we started to notice that the town was finally filling up the pool for the coming summer season. We watched it almost constantly from the hot roof. The black PVC and the torch brought the temperature up past a hundred. During the summer months it would get even hotter. Dennis was in a hurry now, and pushed us harder than before. The pool needed to open, but couldn't until we'd finished the roof. It was almost June and kindergarten would be out in a week, then the rest of the schools near the end of the month. And we still had about a quarter of the roof to torch.

"This is a real treat," Gary said. "A bunch of guys on a hot roof and a whole pool just sitting down there waiting for someone to jump in."

"My uncle–"

"No one wants to hear about your damn uncle."

"What about him?" I asked.

Jeb kicked out another roll of PVC. "There's a company pool about this size on the roof of his office building. You'd never guess it. Just looks like one of those regular skyscrapers. But once you get on top, there's a pool, sauna, racquetball courts, you name it. That way you can come to work and still get some exercise. It's pretty common with commuter jobs at the Toronto Stock Exchange."

"You're full of shit," Gary said.

"So how many interns does he hire every year?"

"Usually up to four or five, depending on the market. He'd have a spot for you if you applied. Actually you'd probably have a better chance than I would, because then he wouldn't worry so much about nepotism. All you would have to do is let me know when you're applying and I'll tell him that you're a friend of mine."

"But I'm not even a business major. He'd want someone more qualified."

"Business doesn't have anything to do with it," he said. "And being from southern Alberta is a real plus. My uncle says that they always have problems with the city-folk ivy leaguers skimming off the top. They'll pay top dollar for a more rural intern because they usually have a better work ethic and they're more honest. Seriously, you'd have a good chance."

Dennis called for a break and Gary was the first to the ladder. I kept talking with Jeb, buoyed a bit by his bullshit.

"Next year, man, riding to work in a company car. Free country club pass, you name it." Jeb climbed down the ladder and I held it, waiting for him to get off.

"Sounds like a kick-ass job," I said. We sat down in the shade next to Gary and Brent. "But why would they hire an intern to make more money than full-timers who have way more experience?"

"Like I said, it just depends on how well you do. Sure you could come out with only 5 to 10K for a summer, but that still beats the hell out of working here. And then there's the first-class treatment. You know, my uncle showed me one of the company cars that picks you up for work every morning. They have fucking *computers* in them. I thought it was a waste until he explained that it was actually more efficient. That way, you could check on the market wherever you were. When you get down to it, just a couple seconds could make the difference between making a pile of money or nothing at all. You just have to change the way you think."

"Like hell," Gary said. "You don't know what the fuck you're talking about."

"Why? Why can't you believe me?"

"Don't even start."

"Just leave it alone," I said.

"No–I want to know. What is it about working for my uncle that bothers you so much?"

"There's no fucking way," Gary said. "You work on a fucking *roofing* crew, for Christ's sake."

Jeb nodded his head, like he was really trying to figure out where Gary was coming from, saying, "Hm, hm." I ate my sandwich and passed Jeb my tapioca. I wasn't about to get involved in the conversation, not at this point. Gary got up and headed to Jimmy's. Jeb watched him leave, shaking his head.

In the afternoon, we were finishing up torching when a girl walked into the pool area. She wore a teal two piece and had bobbed hair and long slender legs that she dipped in the pool, testing the temperature. She looked young, maybe fourteen, but the guys didn't care. We all practically stopped working. Gary rolled out the PVC slowly, like he was counting the rotations. Jeb just smiled. Brent said, "What I wouldn't give for a piece of that."

The girl walked up and down along the pool, then stopped at one of the lounge chairs to sit. How did she get in? I wondered. Dennis came over from torching the cap on the edges, looked, and said, "Quit your gawking, we have work to do." We did, reluctantly. At break she was still there, face to the sun, lying out in front of the pool.

"Should be illegal," Jeb said. "I mean, does she know what she's doing?"

"She knows exactly what she's doing," Gary said. "Bitch wants it."

"She's only a kid," I said.

"She's old enough," Gary said.

Brent laughed. A kind of putt-putt laugh.

"How old do you think she is?" I said.

Gary said, "At least sixteen."

"Not even close," Jeb said. "Thirteen, fourteen, tops."

"Why don't you go find out?" Gary said.

"Why don't you?"

"Hey, I'll make you a deal," Gary said. "If she's closer to thirteen, I shut up and stop bugging you about your fucking uncle. If she's closer to sixteen, then you shut up."

Jeb hesitated a moment, then accepted. Dennis called the end of break, and Jeb was already through the door of the pool house. We scrambled back onto the roof and watched Jeb enter through the men's room door out onto the concrete. His overalls were still covered in tar and his hard hat was on backwards. Jeb walked around the side of the pool and the girl kept her face immobile. Then she cocked her head and lifted up a hand to shield her eyes from the sun. We all watched from the edge of the roof, leaning our elbows on the foot-high cap. Jeb was about fifteen feet away from her when she noticed us on the roofline, gazing down at her like spectators at a cock fight.

"Get back to work," Dennis yelled and we jumped up. Then the girl did a funny thing. She got up out of her chair. Jeb started to talk to her, held out his hand. She backed away and looked up again at all of us. Gary waved. "How about a ride?" he yelled. The girl turned and fled, running along the edge of the pool away from Jeb.

"Are you guys fucking deaf?" Dennis asked. We could hear Dennis behind us, yelling at us to hurry, to get our asses back to work, that we only had a couple of days to get the roof finished. Jeb yelled up from the pool, "I guess she doesn't want to talk to us," and shrugged his shoulders. The girl ran into the women's locker room and Gary bent over to get a better look.

"Fucking beautiful," he said.

At break, all the guys could talk about was the girl in her two piece, what she looked like under her two piece, and what they would do when they found out. Real sick stuff—conversations about the size of their dicks, confessions of how young they'd had it and with whom.

"You guys are disgusting," Jeb said. "That girl was probably only thirteen years old."

"Why don't you just shut the fuck up?" Gary said.

"You guys should look for girls with more class. The kind of girl you could take to a show."

"I take Debbie to shows all the time," Brett said.

"Christ, Brett, I'm not talking movies. I mean like a real live show. With celebrities and stuff."

"Ooooh," I said. "Celebrities." Some of the guys cracked up.

Dennis came over from the truck where he ate lunch and waved his arm. We all put on our hard hats, did up our overalls, and slowly made our way up the ladder, Jeb still jabbering about how to find quality women.

"My uncle's company has these socials downtown. I went to one when I was a kid after a Maple Leafs/Senators game. They had this huge catered room that looked right out onto the ice, and afterwards we went to a restaurant on the CN tower. Imagine going up there, after it's closed to tourists. You got the whole town of Toronto at your feet and the only women you see are these high-class babes with degrees and retirement plans. You know Darla Blake from *Hockey Night in Canada?* She was there. My uncle

introduced me and she said, 'So *you're* Stanton's nephew.'
I about lost it. You know that she's almost six feet tall? And
that's a woman who you can talk to."

"I'd like to do more than that," Brett said.

"You're disgusting," Jeb said.

The next afternoon, the girl was back. This time with a
friend–a younger friend by the looks of it–also wearing a
two piece. She was smaller than the other girl and flat-
chested. The sight of her made everything that Jeb had
said more believable; even Gary was embarrassed. And a
man was there, skimming a fine net across the surface of
the pool while the girls jumped in and out and sunned
themselves on the deck. It was still torturously hot.

"You grunts quit gawking," Dennis yelled. We only had
a day to get the job done and there was still a quarter of
the roof left. Everything was torn off now and we knew
that we'd have to cover the whole roof today if we wanted
to go home at all that evening. Couldn't leave the roof
exposed because of liability–even if the weather report
said sunny weather for the next two months. Dennis
brought on another guy, a machinist who sometimes did
torch work, to do the PVC seams. This was a more specialized job that required a small hand torch to seal the roof
lip and corners, those tight spots that a bigger seam torch
like mine would screw up. Dennis coordinated the last few
steps of getting the insulation and particle board ready for
each new roll of PVC that we put down. It was everything
that we had done earlier compressed into a shorter time
frame and it had to be done right. No room for glitches. By
lunch Gary and Jeb had nailed and screwed in all the insulation and fired up the kettle. With the new guy torching
the roof lip and corners, we were almost caught up to
them and it looked like we should have no problem finishing the rest of the roof by early afternoon. At break, we
sprawled down on the grass near the pool's chain link
fence in the shade of a leafy elm. I chugged a good portion

of my 4-litre thermos, the Gatorade doing its best to replace what I'd sweat on the baking hot roof. The girls were still there, sunning themselves now, in plain view from where we were, under the tree.

"Looks like I won that bet," Jeb said when he sat down.

"That was yesterday," Gary said. "You never asked her. Could be her fucking sister for all we know."

Jeb sighed. Gary got up, stiffly, and marched his way in the direction of Jimmy's. The new guy came down off the ladder, sat with the rest of us in the shade.

"What's his problem?"

"Lost a bet."

The new guy laughed.

After break, the girls and the pool cleaner were gone. The pool was ready to be opened that weekend and the water was clear and inviting. The kettle had warmed up and Dennis pulled the spout over to the roof. Jeb hauled up the two tar-encrusted buckets and put them by the spout. Dennis came up with the stiff mop and Brett followed him, then waited next to the stack of particle board, ready for Dennis to give the order.

"Hot!" Dennis yelled. Jeb pulled the line and waited for the gurgle of tar as it came up and out the spout, into the buckets. But nothing came. He pulled again, harder this time, but there was no familiar gurgle of the tube filling up. Dennis let the mop fall and went back down the ladder. We heard the kettle lid clang open. Smoke spewed out and blew in our direction on the roof. We heard cursing, lots of it. Then the kettle clanged shut again and the smoke disappeared.

"Jeb!"

Jeb hustled down the ladder, taking the buckets with him. Then Dennis re-emerged on the roof, wiping his hands on his overalls. Splatters of tar covered his front like slick leaves. Without a word, he picked up the mop and let it fall in the large empty basin.

I wanted to keep torching, but with the delay down at the kettle, I was almost caught up. I clicked off my torch and closed my tank. Before long, Jeb appeared at the top of the ladder carrying a smoking bucket that he brought over to the basin and dumped in. Dennis swirled the mop around and Jeb went back down the ladder. Gary and Brett waited until Dennis had covered a full rectangle of space, then they lifted the ends of the particle board and laid it on top, exactly in the corner. Dennis waited for them to position it correctly and tamp it down before mopping another spot. A couple more pieces and I'd be ready to torch again. But Dennis had already run out of tar; one bucket wasn't quite enough. Jeb made his way to the top of the ladder, this time breathing heavily. A thick slice of tar was on his overalls, below the knee. Dennis turned his mop upside-down and pried at the stiffening head with his gloves. Jeb dumped the bucket too quickly this time and tar splashed over the edge and onto the roof—luckily not far from where Dennis needed to mop.

"Careful," Dennis said, then dipped his mop in until the fibers were loose, and he mopped the next section for Gary and Brett. They finished the row and I re-lit my torch. The particle board would be good for a couple more rolls of PVC cap. Next time I looked up, Dennis had switched Gary and Jeb, but they were behind and it was getting close to quitting time and we still had a couple rows left. With the kettle spout busted, we were going to be there longer, and that pissed everyone off.

Dennis called a late break at 5:00, when we were usually slathering a couple lines of tar paper with hot to temporarily seal the old roof to the new one on our way out. Everyone was exhausted, except for me and the new guy. Racing up and down the ladder carrying buckets of tar had worn them all out, even after switching. And the usual breaks of putting in new tar blocks to be melted in the kettle made for delays. We were going to be getting time-and-a-half for our work, but not even that mattered to Gary,

Jeb, and Brett who were covered with flecks of tar from the sloshing buckets.

"Come here," Dennis said. We all got to our feet and walked to where he stood, over tar that was oozing into the grass and partially onto the concrete sidewalk surrounding the building. "What the fuck is this?" Dennis asked.

"Tar," Jeb said.

"No shit, Sherlock," Dennis said. He took off his hard hat and wiped his head with his sleeve. He turned around and kicked a dried chunk of tar skittering out onto the concrete. "You going to do something about it?" He looked straight at Jeb.

"I could," Jeb started. "But I wasn't the one who spilled it—wouldn't it be more fair to have whoever spilled it clean it up?"

Dennis just stared at Jeb. "If you worked as much as you talked, I'd be a goddamn millionaire," he said.

We worked the same as we had before the break until I had finished torching my seam. Then Dennis sent Jeb down to clean the tar off the concrete with a wire brush and solvent. Dennis waved me over to help lay the fiberboard. Gary ran hot for us and we started laying the last line, a task that took a while longer because we had to cut each piece to fit with a utility knife. We were right against the edge of the roof now and the ladder poked up in the middle, so all that Gary had to do was dump the hot in the basin when he got to the top.

We were in the last corner when we heard it. I was kneeling on a piece of fiberboard, cutting out two lines to fit the last couple angles. Dennis had already mopped the tar and it was cooling, waiting for my piece. Brett and I both were tamping it in when we heard a dull thump like a struck timpani. Then Jeb screamed. We all craned over the edge and saw Jeb running in the parking lot wearing a thick swath of black tar from his overall pocket to his shoulder blades, his arms straight out. The fabric clung to him like a wet t-shirt. We saw the overturned bucket, Gary on the ground next to it, looking as shocked as we were. Dennis ran to the ladder and shimmied down, missing most of the steps, then sprinted to his truck, opened it, and went after Jeb with a fire extinguisher. Parts of Jeb's clothing were smoldering. Brett and I were transfixed by the scene. Only Gary seemed conscious of what had happened. He ran over to where Dennis had smothered Jeb with foam and the two of them helped Jeb to Dennis' truck. Dennis peeled out, leaving black streaks on the pavement.

We all made our way down the ladder.

"Fucking moron," Gary said. "Fucking dropped the bucket." He was shaking as he patted his pockets for his smokes, then he lit up, still swearing.

We finished capping the roof, Brett and Gary both taking off before Dennis's Chevy rolled slowly back into the lot. It was almost 7:00. We were hungry and dehydrated, but the project was finished and our torches and tanks were on the lawn, ready to go. Dennis explained how it happened, that it was Gary who had dropped the bucket on his way up the ladder, sending the hot onto Jeb who was crouched over, cleaning tar off the cement. "Didn't even need any more hot," he said, like it was a waste. He went up on the roof with us and surveyed the finished job—the parallel lines of PVC glistening where the sun struck it, interrupted only by the shadows of heating vents and the roof lip. "One big fucking job," Dennis said.

Jeb got worker's comp for the rest of the summer. He visited the crew once, three weeks later. He looked the same as always, though when he lifted the back of his shirt, we saw the bandages and shrinking areas where the tar had puckered the skin in third degree burns. He would have scars.

"Still get paid," he said.

We were all still on the crew and I was worried about Jeb and Gary turning on each other. But Gary apologized.

He treated Jeb like he was a visiting dignitary. Jeb seemed to like the attention. Gary showed him around the elementary school gymnasium we were working on–another large job that we started as soon as school was out. He introduced Jeb to the three other guys working with us, mostly temps or students looking to make a couple bucks. Gary told Jeb how we had already gone through four other grunts a week before. One of them was an overweight kid with a lisp. Gary called him "blubber butt" to his face until the kid left two days later.

"The guys were fucking pansies," Gary said. Jeb laughed and told us how the rest of the summer was paid for, that he was reading all the books he needed to for his fall classes during the day so that he could keep his time open for scoping babes. "They pay for everything," he said. "Royal fucking treatment."

"Shit, man," Brent said. "You said it."

Gary said that Jeb was the luckiest guy in the world.

SHOOT THE MOON

As a lawyer, I've learned how important it is to tell the truth.

My story begins in childhood, before I really knew Sweet Dent. I grew up in Ridgeview, a town settled by Mormon polygamists whom the Canadian government welcomed to the area because of their knowledge of irrigation. The vestiges of their industry remained in Ridgeview in the form of homes, churches, and a system of canals that extended south of town, past our place, a block after the pavement had turned to gravel. One of the original canals was still there, unused. It was flanked by the old golf course, a name we neighborhood kids used to describe the adjacent four or five acres of abandoned land. The old golf course, like the canal, had long ago submitted to the will of the prairie, the cyclical onslaught of wind and snow. Left were a shack of graying wood, two prongs of a fence, and miles of gopher holes and garter snakes. It got the name "the old golf course" for the golf balls that had claimed the area, driven from the suburban homes on the other side of the canal. These balls seemed to me to have fallen from the sky; some were old and caked with dirt, half-buried in the prairie soil. Uncovering them was like being on an archaeological dig, and I amassed the golf balls in piles before the topsoil covered them up completely. I knew one great golfer in the area: Sweet Dent. He had been one of the founders of the 9-hole Ridgeview golf course, and I often delivered to him the golf balls that I cleaned and put in an old egg carton and he gave me a dollar.

He told me stories.

"There was a golf course as old as time before the pioneers came," he said. "It was the oldest golf course of all, God's golf course." He made a great straight man and I was horribly naive. The only way I'd know if he was telling the truth or not was when his wife was there, or my scoutmaster Reg. They laughed like crazy even though Sweet frequently repeated himself and never cracked a smile, but I just listened to his stories, yearning to believe, not wanting to unmask him, to declare him a fraud. He told me about God's golf course, how in the early years on the prairie, large boulders dotted the countryside. The prairie was the putting green and the boulders were missed putts. He described the boulders in such detail—so huge that some farmers just left them in their fields, like giant dolmens, protruding from the plains in the middle of their crops—that I believed every word.

One time I dropped off a box of golf balls and Reg was there in the living room. Sweet had a two bedroom bungalow that he and his wife shared until she died some years later. The front room housed a huge wood-burning stove, a couple recliners, and the T.V. When company came, they got out folding chairs and a card table. Reg stood from one of the chairs when I stepped through the door with my carton of carefully polished old golf balls.

Sweet inspected the lot, holding each ball about two feet away so that he could see them clearly. "An old Titleist," he said. "Good shape." He placed the balls on a shelf next to a trophy of a golfer following through on his swing. "The Ridgeview open," he said, then pointed to himself, "Champ." The "Ridgeview Open," as he called it, sounded impressive, but Reg and Sweet's wife Doris laughed. "Oh, dear," Doris said, in her waning Welsh accent. "Stop teasing."

"Always teasing," Sweet said. "She accuses me, you know. Ever since I met her in London. Never believes me, even when I tell her the truth."

"That's because you never tell the truth," Reg said. He laughed and Sweet shook his head.

"I've a mind to throw you out of my house," Sweet said. They both laughed.

Sweet got up from his chair and pointed to the door. "That has your name on it. And the back of my shoe. Send you out the door into the snow."

"It's summer, dear," Doris said.

"They don't listen to me," Sweet said, sitting back down. He bent over, gave me a confiding look. "It's because they're getting old." He pointed to his head, moved his finger around in a circle. "Crazy," he said.

I started going to the Dents' every week with Reg to play Hearts. I suppose that I could rationalize my visits, say that I was bored during the summer, that I turned to hanging out with my scoutmaster and the Dents because the rest of my friends drove combine for their fathers or worked moving irrigation pipes. Most folks around Ridgeview would probably need that sort of rationalization. I know that I got my share of comments about my visits, as though I were some charitable soul for giving up my precious summer time. Sweet had a reputation. He was one of the only Catholics in a town full of Mormons and he had several eccentricities. Once, when I was with my cousin Ben buying Slurpees at Jimmy's, we saw Sweet cruise by on his adult tricycle with a couple bags of groceries in the wire mesh basket out front. Sweet's bike was the only one like it in town and he had ridden it as long as I could remember. I had never thought it unusual until my cousin pointed it out.

"Look at the nut-job on the trike," Ben said.

"That's Sweet," I said.

"Sweet?"

"That's his name."

I asked Sweet about his trike the next week over a game of Hearts. I was young and tried to shoot the moon by distracting everyone with questions or observations. If people were interested enough, they'd stop paying attention to the cards, not notice that I was playing low, counting until I knew that I had the highest cards in any suit. "Why do you always ride your bike?" I asked.

"A serious question," Sweet said. "You're trying to shoot."

"I am not," I said.

"He doesn't have a driver's license," Doris said.

"You don't have a driver's license?"

"He's trying to change the subject," Sweet said. "You don't fool me. You watch his cards."

Doris said, "He never needed one."

"But you have a car."

"I drive it," Reg said. "I'm their chauffeur."

It seemed odd to me, but I guess it was something that they had worked out. For emergencies and whatnot.

"I used to drive until I had leg problems," Doris said.

"What's wrong with your legs?"

"Not trustworthy."

"You never know which way they're going to go," Sweet said. "Have a mind of their own."

I led the ace of spades.

Sweet said, "I told you. What's the matter with you people? I'll get the grenadine."

We put down our cards and waited for Sweet to stop clanking around in the kitchen. Finally, he brought out a tin tray of ginger ale and grenadine. I relished these breaks. For all of Sweet's and Doris's idiosyncrasies and apparent poverty, they had great taste when it came to desserts and non-alcoholic drinks. They made a point of never drinking around me—I was still a minor, and Mormon to boot. The grenadine and Canada Dry mixture was one of my favorites. They always managed to produce a bottle of the red syrupy stuff and at least a plate of ginger-

snaps or shortbread cookies. Sometimes they had home-
made ice cream, churned from a vintage crankshaft model
made from cedar and steel. Sweet flexed his forearms
when I asked how he got the ice cream so smooth. "I hook
these up to the crank and put them on automatic."
    When Sweet came back with the drinks, I shot the moon.

School started in the fall and I had less and less time to
visit the Dents, though Reg would still encourage me to
visit when I could. I found that I had talent in shop. My
shop teacher, Mr. Rigby, noticed that I had an eye for
detail, so he put me and another student, Jon Tucker, on
the lathe. At first we just glued pieces of wood together,
put them on the spindle, then gouged the hell out of them.
Gradually we developed our own expertise; Jon liked
bowls, I liked goblets. I made one with a ring that you split
off and left hanging around the stem like an ankle bracelet,
and then a fluted champagne glass out of cherry that
required me to keep the tools extra sharp to get down
deep in the gullet. I made several more goblets out of various hardwoods and my mother proudly put them up on
our mantle, so that they were visible to visitors. "My son
works on the wood lathe," she'd say. They made excellent
gifts and they gradually disappeared from the mantle and
ended up with relatives or friends from school. A week
before Christmas, I decided to give my favorite goblet, the
one with the ringed stem, to the Dents.
    I put the goblet in a box with a self-adhesive ribbon on
top. I wrapped just the top portion of the box so that it
looked entirely covered but fit snugly over the bottom
half. Sweet was there at the door when I knocked. He was
singing "Edelweiss," slowly, just the chorus, over and over,
scooping from note to note.
    "This is for you." I put the box in his hands.
    "Come in, come in."
    He took me into the living room but didn't invite me to
sit down. Doris' recliner was vacant. Sweet stopped in the

middle of the room. He started shredding the wrapping paper and the box came apart in his hands, like two halves of a clamshell. He grabbed the goblet lightly by the stem and held it up in front of him like one of my golf balls. "Beautiful," he kept saying, "beautiful," barely audible.

"Where's Doris?" I asked.

"Gone to visit her sister." Sweet placed the goblet on his mantle next to a picture of a man, woman, and child with a little boy. "See that boy there?"

"Yes."

"He's your age."

The parents and the kid had older, fuller hairstyles, not too unlike the pictures of my parents when they were younger. The man had large bristly sideburns and wore amber-tinted glasses. The boy was in a two-toned velvet shirt, wide open at the collar. The mother wore a flowery blouse with pink accents, green vines curving in a repeating pattern. The boy looked familiar, so I asked Sweet about him.

"He plays basketball. Inside all the time. Stinking and sweaty. Just like his father." His arm wobbled as he reached toward the picture and knocked it over. "They live in Lethbridge. Doris will phone and tell them when she gets home from her sister's. She'll phone them up."

It was then that I noticed the faint smell of alcohol on his breath.

"They never visit, you know. You're a good boy. You come and visit us. You made a goblet with your own hands. Better than my own grandson."

Sweet stepped towards me and lifted his arm like a blind man reaching for a handhold. He found my shoulder and started to pull me in, to hug me. I became incredibly tense–this was so different from the jovial, sarcastic Sweet I knew–but I let him hold on. I could smell the alcohol strongly now and his skin was damp with perspiration that seeped through his work shirt.

"I have to go," I said after he released me.

"A good boy," he said.

School started up again in January. Though I had found
the real reason for Doris' absence, I refrained from visiting
the Dents. Looking back now, I wonder why. Whenever
Reg phoned me to tell me that he was going over "in a
couple days or so" I always said that I had something
going on, which was partially true if I thought about it long
enough. I was busy with homework and I was in the spring
play—the Canadian debut of *Big River*—though I had
merely a bit part in the chorus and only practiced on Tues-
days and Thursdays. The next time Reg phoned me, he
said, "You've heard about Doris, haven't you?" Then I told
him about my visit with Sweet before Christmas and how
he said she was visiting her sister. "She's in the hospital,"
Reg said. "Her mind is going and Sweet isn't taking good
enough care of her." I didn't know what to say to that.
Why had Sweet lied? I liked things to add up. I told myself
that I would go and visit Doris, had to. She would be
happy to see me, I was sure; but as the pace of the semester accelerated through spring, I failed even to phone. In
the meantime, I was also socializing with a crowd in Lethbridge. Two of the *Big River* cast members were from
Lethbridge and once at a party, they introduced me to the
basketball player, Sweet's grandson, Cole. He was tall and
lanky and didn't physically resemble Sweet, but I knew
from the picture that it was him. Same squarish head, and,
ironically, the same confrontational sense of humor.

"I used to visit your grandparents," I told him. Don't
ask me why I put it in the past tense. Perhaps it was my
concern that his family, for some reason, had elected not
to visit them.

"How's the geezer doing?"

"Fine, I guess. Doris is in the hospital."

"Yeah, I saw her last week."

"You did?"

Something about my tone must have suggested surprise. All I could think of were the damp arms of Sweet
around me, the alcohol, Doris' empty chair.

"Yes, we did."

"Was Sweet there?"

"He never is. Least not when we're there."

"Why not?"

"He and my father don't get along."

"Oh," I said.

I decided to visit the Dents again—this time at the hospital to see Doris with Sweet and Reg. Doris remembered my name, but not much else. The words came out syntactically jumbled in her quiet Welsh lilt. I could no longer rely on her to cue Sweet's jests, but she seemed happy enough that we were there.

"The light's on, but nobody's home," Sweet said. Right in front of Doris.

"It's not that bad."

"She's a nut case, my dear sweet nut case. Loony as they come." Sweet patted her shoulder.

"Oh, you're abonible. Abobinable. Oh, dear, oh."

"She understands everything. It's when she talks that it comes out crazy," Sweet said.

"Not crazy," she said.

"There you go."

"It was good to see you," I said.

After saying our goodbyes to Doris and Sweet, Reg stated the obvious, that she was getting old. "She's on her way out," he said, like she was a fading fashion.

Reg's words proved prophetic. By the end of the summer, she was dead.

I went to the University of Lethbridge in the fall, a step that almost signaled the end of this story. I saw Sweet often enough immediately after Doris's death, but then my visits dwindled. I attended the funeral, was there for Sweet's grotesque outbreak when he complained that the mortician had made Doris up "like a hooker." And Sweet still ran his errands around town on his adult tricycle.

But my life moved on. I had classes, exams, professors, and a social life. About the only time I thought about Sweet was at the University of Lethbridge basketball games where Cole played point guard. I would watch him dribble up the court, waiting for a pick to open up a lane for a drive to the basket, and think how Sweet would like to see this. Then I'd turn back to the game and drink my pop and eat my bag of chips.

But in the spring, my father told me that Sweet's usually low-maintenance heart was beginning to give him troubles. I knew that I would have to go back. I was in the last stretch of my fourth year at the U of L and I had just received admission to McGill for a degree in law. I was still uneasy about my decision to go. A talk with Sweet, I thought, might help me solidify my plans. It was all I could think about for days. With Sweet's heart about to conk out and my plans for the future beginning to waver, it wasn't long before I found myself in front of Sweet's bungalow, one hand in my pocket, the other knocking hard.

"I thought you were the police," he said when he answered the door. "I should have known better. Come in."

The house was unchanged except for a Doris shrine that had replaced the photograph of Cole's family. In the center was a black-and-white picture of her in an oval gilded gold frame. Doris had her hair back with her head tilted slightly to the side. She wasn't smiling, and she exuded a sort of poise and class that made me wonder how she had ended up with Sweet. The shrine had other pictures of him and Doris at their home with Doris sitting in her recliner. There was also a calligraphy copy of a love poem and the obituary that Reg had helped Sweet to write before Doris' funeral. Looking at the carefully arranged shrine, I imagined Sweet as an uxorious husband, a man who doted on his wife, submitted to her, loved her. I remembered the good-natured teasing that concealed Sweet's adulation. But then I thought of his moments of excess or indulgence, his jokes at Doris' expense and I

wondered who really submitted to whom. I realized that I
had no real knowledge about the daily workings of their
lives, of what went on behind the closed doors of more
than fifty years of marriage.

"How are you, Sweet?"

Sweet settled down in Doris' easy chair and nudged a
crystal dish of sugar-free candies wrapped in cellophane. I
took one and un-crinkled the wrap until the candy
dropped into my lap like a purple jewel. "Whenever someone asks me that, it makes me feel old."

"Sorry."

"That's OK. I am, you know."

"What?"

"Old." Sweet opened his mouth and brayed. Very
unexpected. I suppose I hadn't truly heard Sweet laugh
before. He had always relied on others to pick up his
jokes, perpetual laughers like Reg or Doris. But neither of
them was here now. Sweet needed something to fill the
space, to let me know how to interpret his humor, so he
chose to do it himself, wheezing like a sick animal.

"You're not that old."

"Are you kidding me?" he said. "I'm as old as they
come. Liable to drop dead any minute."

"Whatever you say."

Silence. Sweet got up and walked to the kitchen, yelled
back, "What'll you drink?"

"Do you still have grenadine?"

"Sure thing." He came back with a chilled liter of
Canada Dry and a bottle of grenadine. He put the tray
down and we mixed our own virgin drinks, then drank
them, soaking up the silence. I felt more inclined to speak
then, so when Sweet asked me how my studies were
going, I let the words come out. I told Sweet about school,
everything that had happened in the past four years. I told
him about his grandson Cole's basketball games and
about the parties I'd go to and how I planned on attend-
ing McGill in the fall. Then I got carried away. I gave him

summaries of my preliminary reading list, theory from the
Greeks to the 19th century. I explained the rudiments of
the Socratic method and I outlined my aspirations to
eventually become a lawyer proficient in French criminal
and English civil law. Sweet kept abreast of my conversation and sipped his ginger ale and rocked slightly in his
La-Z-Boy. I didn't know what to make of his silence, so I
kept talking. Was this some sort of silent approbation? But
when he finally did interrupt, it wasn't with any direction
about my future.

"You saw my grandson play?" he asked.

"Saw almost every game," I said.

Sweet put down his drink and brushed his hands
quickly together. "I'll put some wood in the stove," he said.
He opened the stove grate and warmth seeped into the
room. It was evening and the spring was as unpredictable
as ever, with a recent cold stretch and blizzard followed by
a Chinook wind and then cold again. One day I counted
four distinct types of weather: drizzle, hail, snow, and sun-
shine. A four-season day. Sweet tossed in two logs and
nudged them with a poker. "What's my grandson like?"

Sweet kept his back to me; whatever was in the stove
was worth looking at. I said that he was doing well, as far
as I knew. Sweet sighed and closed the stove grate and
came back and sat down.

"He's a nice enough guy," I said. "Tall."

"He's like his father, isn't he? That's why you're hedging."

"Hedging?"

"You don't want to tell me that he's a sorry excuse for a
human being."

"I don't know Cole's father," I said. "But Cole isn't that
bad."

Then Sweet did a strange thing. He walked over to the
mantle and picked up the goblet that I had given him
years ago. It was still as I remembered it: the mouth was
almost tulip-shaped, and the ring still hung around the
stem like a thin wooden bangle. He shuffled back to the

stove and creaked open the grate with his free hand. He sat down on a stool and held the goblet close to the fire. "Prove it," he said.

"Prove what?"

"Prove to me that Cole is a decent sort of person. Tell me something to show that he's tops."

"I don't know any stories," I said. And I didn't. Cole for me was a guy I saw only on occasion, a local basketball icon that I had talked to four or five times if that. I knew what I read about in the paper: there was a controversy about the Medicine Hat game where he'd elbowed that guy in the stomach and I knew a thing or two about how he treated his friends, but that was it.

Sweet stared absently at the fire and twirled the ring of the goblet around its stem like a wooden hula-hoop. He held the goblet close to the oven's mouth and I could see the reflections of the coals on the polyurethane finish. I recalled how hard it had been to get all of the bubbles out of that finish, without any brushstrokes. Our shop teacher didn't like us using the pneumatic sprayer for small pieces like goblets, so we used either foam brushes or ones with fine bristles to get the finish smooth.

"Sure you do," he said.

I racked my brain for something that I could tell Sweet, something that would alleviate his grief and keep him from throwing my goblet into the fire.

"What do you want to know, Sweet?"

"Tell me a story," he said.

I did remember one thing—a time when I was almost out of money and I was living on potatoes. I had concocted just about everything imaginable out of the miraculous tubers and had rationed them out until the end of the month—a couple of potatoes a day: potato puree, potato salad (minus eggs and green onions), grated hash browns. With my last five bucks, I went to the local Safeway to get another bag and then about a pound of hamburger for protein. I ran into Cole at the check-out. He had a full cart, a regular horn of plenty, things I couldn't imagine ever buying. He had pop-tarts, ready-made dinners with names like beef bourguignon or salmon penne, and about three different kinds of soft drinks in six-packs. He was still bagging his groceries when I went through with my literal meat-and-potatoes meal. I had calculated the total out in my head but I had forgotten about GST. When the teller rang me up, I was 37 cents short. I didn't know what to do. I held out my five, was about to ask her to take out the hamburger, when Cole opened his wallet, said, "How much you need?" Fifty cents later, I was home to cook my lunch.

"He bought me groceries once," I said. "When I was out of money and living off potatoes." It was a stretch, but close enough to the truth.

Sweet thought for a second. "So he thinks he can buy you. So what."

Sweet's assessment didn't seem fair; it was obvious that Cole was wealthier than I was, but that didn't mean he was buying me off. Maybe I made it sound too generous? Like I was at some soup kitchen and he was a celebrity coming for a photo shoot saying *yes I do care for the poor.* Or maybe it didn't sound generous enough? Sweet still held the goblet near the open grate. But I didn't know any more stories, nothing that could prove his grandson was "tops." So I did the next best thing: I made it up.

"I do remember one time he came caroling with a group of my friends to an old folks home in Lethbridge. We went with a group of my friends who sang well, and even though he didn't know all the songs, he came along anyway."

Sweet fingered the goblet, his back still to me.

"They loved him there because he was so tall. He had to crouch to go through one of the doorways and almost hit his head on a piece of mistletoe. He blushed and one of the old ladies said, 'He's up for grabs now, girls,' and everyone laughed."

The ring twirled and twirled.

"So I was worried he'd be all upset or embarrassed that he came along. I was feeling a little guilty, you know, since I was the one who talked him into it. But then he surprised us by going up to one of the ladies and giving her a kiss right on the cheek. It was a woman who was sitting in a wheelchair over near the Christmas tree. She smiled and patted him on the arm, then we finished caroling and went to another home. We must have caroled for two or three hours before people's voices started giving out. I'd have to say that's one of the better memories I have about your grandson. Really is a great guy."

Sweet turned around, shaking his head and resting the cup on his knee.

"Well?" I asked.

He sighed, then tossed the goblet into the fire. I could hear the finish crackling, igniting the rest of the piece. He closed the grate shut.

"You're a liar," he said. "Get out of my house before I throw you out." He stood up.

I was stunned.

"You think I'm too old? I can do it, you know. Get out. Now."

I got to my feet and grabbed my coat from the nail in the hallway. Sweet stayed within three feet of me the whole time and followed me out. When I closed the door, I looked behind me, and he was peering through the slats of his mini-blinds. I walked briskly down the driveway and pointed myself home, toward my studies, my future, and my eventual profession.

FRANCIS THE GIANT

It was the third day of my sleep deprivation experiment and I was about to castrate a herd of cattle with Francis Goodrich, the dumbest kid in my grade. I had started the experiment as part of our grade 12 Biology class for Mr. Charles, who put Francis with me because he thought he could use the popularity points. "He needs friends, Darcy," he said to me privately. Francis was about five-two and he had a harelip and he lisped so much that when he talked more than a minute at a time, spittle balled up at the corners of his mouth. He liked DC comics and rap and last year he performed at our annual air band competition doing MC Hammer's "Too Legit to Quit" by himself. He messed up Hammer's hand signals and when he jump-crossed his legs and unwound, he fell over and everyone laughed. In the halls kids called him space cadet, shit-for-brains, fuckface Francis, and a hundred other things that were stupid and not nice. I was a football player, a running back with 200 yards in rushing already this season, and I was smart. I took on Francis reluctantly, like I was hoofing it up a mountain, shouldering a pack of rocks.

"Stand on your head," I said. We were at my house, in the back family room, playing video games. It was almost morning. For our experiment, we had apparatuses set up all over the room to test things like our reflexes or ability to read. Our hypothesis was this: that sleep deprivation could mimic intoxication. So far our results didn't add up, mostly because Francis' performance on routine tasks was so erratic. The reading test wouldn't work because I had to help him through the words even when he wasn't tired. One speed test counted the number of times you could press a buzzer in thirty seconds. All you had to do was put your finger down as fast as you could: "Buzz, buzz, buzz." Francis' attempts were even and slow, about a third as fast as mine were. "Faster," I would say and Francis pressed the button slow and hard until the plastic buzzer snapped.

"Stand on your head," I said again. Francis was nodding off. "You need to get some blood to your brain." We were playing Gauntlet, a Sega game, going on five hours. It was a four-player shooter and Francis' Valkyrie was bumping into the same wall over and over, a sharp, Harpy-like "Aieee" coming from the tube each time a goblin rammed the Valkyrie in the side. I elbowed Francis. "Did I die again?" The Valkyrie vanished in a digitized puff just as he woke up.

"Stand on your fucking head," I said.

Francis put his head on the floor and tried in vain to throw his feet up against the wall. In Gauntlet, my Elf shot through a barrage of monsters, ghosts, demons, and sorcerers. Without another player I was getting hammered. I moved my Elf around, looking for some health to carry me through the level, but as I did so, I tripped a hidden lock to a door and literally hundreds of monsters swarmed to where I battled in the middle of the screen. "Fuck it," I said, and tossed the paddle to the ground and punched the power on the TV. That's when I could hear Francis snoring.

A couple hours later, Dad phoned saying that he was down a hand and he needed me out at the ranch. He didn't care that I'd been up three days. The cattle wouldn't wait. I didn't mind hard work; I was a big guy, heavy around the chest with a head that squared into my neck. But I preferred ramming my body into people, not steers, and I usually got out of helping at the ranch on account of football.

"Should I come?" Francis asked. I had a hard time picturing Francis working cattle but I wasn't going to leave him by himself all day. Plus maybe there was a way we could work it into our research, a test of what would happen when someone was on the job and sleep deprived. "No way I'm leaving you here," I said.

I made Francis drive the pickup all the way to the ranch to keep him awake. We headed out past the Alberta Wheat Pool elevators and Wolf Creek Hutterite Colony, and Francis drove slow but jittery. Twice he jerked the wheel when we hit a patch of new gravel and the truck fishtailed a bit and I yelled "Don't overcorrect" and then we were back on the road, the pickup sending up a smoke-screen of dust behind it.

"Thanks for not killing us," I said when we pulled up. Francis put the truck into park and we slammed the truck doors and walked around a silver Quonset to where our property opened up to the coulees. We could hear the cattle and the lawnmower hum of a couple four-wheelers. The sun was warm and the prairie brome grass bent in the wind. I was dead tired.

"Bosco and Parkins are trying to round up all the calves," I said. "I'll see where my dad is." First thing Francis did was sit cross-legged on the ground. He plopped down like a dropping sack of flour. "Get up," I said. I helped him to his feet and he wobbled for a bit then held steady. I wondered if he was right for this, if it had been a mistake to bring him out. Our research showed that sleep deprivation could mess you up bad. The first documented experiment we found was in France in 1894 when a Madame de Manacéine killed a pack of dogs by keeping them awake for thirteen days. When she cut the dogs open, they all had these little hemorrhages in their brains. Later experiments we researched had less dramatic results: occasional hallucinations or drug-like buzzes. If Francis hemorrhaged from his brain and died I wondered if the world would be any worse off. I couldn't leave him so I pushed him forward, scanning the horizon for my dad, but it wasn't long before I could feel my body gradually shutting off too. Last thing I wanted was for Dad to find me conked out on the grass. In a last ditch effort, I thought of the *Nightmare on Elm Street* movies we watched the night before, about Freddy with his knives for hands, people slashed and hacked and screaming for just falling asleep. But the psychology wasn't working. Finally, I sat down. The scent of the coulees and cow pies and the soft summer air were doing a number on me.

"What do you think you're doing?" I heard the words but didn't know their source until Dad knocked me over onto the ground and my legs unfolded and I pushed myself up on my elbows and shielded my eyes from the sun. Parkins and Bosco were there now, lean and pissed, with their hockey hair and dinner-plate-sized belt buckles and their camouflaged four wheelers. My dad was a big man in his own way. He wore suspenders over a flannel shirt that strained against his gut and he had my same neck and shoulders. He said, "I don't have time to babysit." Then the three of them headed over to the cattle run with their backs to us. I scrambled to my feet and kicked Francis to get him going. My two-minute or two-second nap had me ready to go but Francis was still sluggish.

The cattle run was a good-sized corral with a maze of fencing on one end leading up to a cradle that looked like a giant waffle iron. The cradle held the cattle still while Dad and Parkins made quick work of the calf's testicles and budding horns. We were supposed to chase each calf into the maze that led to the chute. If the calf wouldn't go, Bosco pushed it and lifted his arms like he was doing the wave at a baseball game, yelling "H'yah, h'yah." The spooked calf sprinted through the maze until it reached the end where the cradle's jaws clamped around its body and head.

"Get that son of a bitch," Bosco said. One calf wasn't going near the chute's entrance. From the smell of the burning flesh or the distant calf bawling, he knew that what awaited him on the other end wasn't a bed of alfalfa. Bosco cornered the calf to get it going then I chased it through. We could hear my Dad and Parkins on the other side clamping the cradle shut, immobilizing the calf. The calf bawled and they pushed another one through. Francis straddled the fence, just watching, until Bosco waved him down.

"Ever wrestled a calf before?"

Little 5-foot-2 shit-for-brains Francis now had the perpetual look of a somnambulist: cloudy eyes, sallow complexion, head drooping like a wilted flower. Francis wrestle a calf? He jumped off the fence and readied himself. Bosco was already in one corner of the feedlot, his arms up. I held out along the flank in case calves bolted from the herd, then we drove the cattle into the corral. The first few took their time, pawing the ground, mulling around until the run narrowed and they got forced into single file. One calf pushed away and fled, misdirected toward me. I pounced on its side, bringing it down with a kind of headlock until the calf's legs buckled. Then I let it go, slapping its hindquarters like it was a fellow teammate on the football field.

"Francis, to your right!"

Francis turned just as a calf shied past Bosco and headed straight toward him. He scooted out of the way, one hand in his pocket, a confused matador without his cape. "Bring it down, shithead," I said. I walked over to where Francis was still sidestepping the calf. Then, just before I could get to him, Francis threw his body onto the calf and it took off like it had been shot. Francis had the form right—he tried to grab on, laying into its side to bring its head back and down—but the calf had too much forward momentum and the kid was just too small. It dragged Francis through cow pies and mud and threw him against the fence. Francis rolled onto his side and then got up on his hands and knees. Bosco had the calf now and he funneled it into the run.

"Don't wrestle them if you don't know how," Bosco said. I walked over to where Francis was now kneeling and holding one hand to his side. For some reason the kid was really starting to piss me off.

"What does this got to do with the experiment?" Francis said.

"You don't know anything, shithead. Occupational testing. This is our practicum. *Can a rancher still put in a good day's work?* Only one real way to find out. Get up."

"I don't think I can do this."

"You got to do something, shithead. There is no way in hell I'm going to let you sleep again."

"Stop calling me that."

"What did you say?"

"Stop calling me shithead."

"You want me to stop calling you shithead, shithead?"

"Yeah," Francis said.

Francis was still kneeling beneath me, humble and small. I kicked a cow pie and chunks of it landed in Francis's lap.

"Stop it," he said.

"There's some shit for you shithead," I said. I kept kicking. Some hit Francis on the arm, some square in the chest. A chunk sat in Francis's lap like a half loaf of bread. He picked it up and threw it at my pants.

"You better have not just thrown that at me shithead," I said.

I couldn't stop myself. Francis was everything I wasn't: small, afraid, weak. On a normal day I wouldn't have wasted a moment with this worm lying in the mud. But he rankled me. Maybe it was the fatigue, the intoxication of sleeplessness, but I felt like I could go as far as I wanted to. I grabbed Francis's arm and pulled him up just far enough that I could hit him in the face. He fell down, a mess of muddy clothes and cow pies. He started to cry.

"What did you do that for?" Bosco said. He momentarily stopped running the calves and grabbed me by the arm.

I would've pummeled Francis, would've smashed his face into the ground but Bosco held me until I calmed down. Francis palmed his cheek and jaw. He lay down in the shit. His cries sounded almost like coughs as he exhaled and inhaled mucus. His body started to shake. "Lay off, man," Bosco said. I shrugged. I tried to help Francis to his feet, but as soon as I touched him he convulsed. "C'mon, Francis," I said. He still wouldn't budge. "Shit," I said. "Some experiment."

I left Francis there to sleep it off.

Bosco seemed to have the rest of the calves under control, so I went to help with branding and castrating. I felt as energized and awake as I'd ever been. We weren't the first people to rely on work to deprive us of sleep. The most famous was in 1959 when a DJ for a New York radio station stayed awake for 200 hours in a glass booth in Times Square. The guy, Tripp was his name, was working to raise money for charity. He did his show the whole week just sitting there with his microphone in the glass booth like a lone guppy in a fish tank.

Parkins had his hand on a lever, waiting for Bosco to run the next calf through. Soon enough, a calf barreled down through the chute and into the cradle. Parkins pulled the cradle shut so that both sides clamped over the calf. Then he and my dad branded, castrated, and dehorned it. Dad seemed to enjoy castration the most, slicing the upper half of the calf's scrotum with a scalpel and working the testes into a bucket. Then he sterilized the wound and his scalpel and fingers in another bucket of rubbing alcohol, letting his rubber-gloved hands drip dry. Parkins did the horns and the brand. He tried to stand so that the wind blew the stench of burning flesh away. He had an electric brander that was white-hot in seconds and burned nice pink lines into the hide, through the skin and hair. The dehorning took longer. They used an electric dehorner that looked like a police baton that was hollow at one end.

They fit the baton over the small lump of a horn until it had burned into the skull, killing the horn. The calf bawled and then everyone moved out of the way and Parkins opened up the cradle enough so that the calf could get out.

Pretty soon, they had me do the cradle.

"Wait till the head's through, then clamp it shut."

We took our places, me on the end of the lever and to secure the latch and anti-kick bar. I could hear Bosco hooting as he forced the calves through the chute. A calf came through and we caught it. I pulled down on the lever until its hide ridged up through the bars and then clamped the latch shut. I didn't even have to move the bar to keep the calf's legs from kicking. The calf had walked into the cradle's jaws perfectly.

Parkins pointed to the round lumps on either side of the calf's head and said, "This one's gonna hurt like a bitch."

Dad's bucket of balls grew. After another hour we took a break. Before Dad covered up the bucket, we all had a look even though it gave me the willies. They were walnut-sized, covered by a thin translucent skin.

"What's that?" It was Francis, bleary-eyed, one arm rubbing his elbow.

Neither of us had seen him coming. Parkins had one testis between his thumb and index finger. He pretended like he put it in his mouth, then he opened his hands and the testis was gone. He reached behind my ear and pulled it out, then dropped it in my hand. I thought I was going to gag. But I kept my composure, said, "What does it look like shithead?" Francis shrugged and I dropped the testicle in the bucket. It sounded like stepping in a puddle.

"Balls," Francis said. "Cow balls."

Parkins said, "He's not as dumb as he looks."

After break, we returned to our same positions, like we were automatons at a factory with specialized tasks. What kept me awake at first–the slicing, the smell, the primal-

sounds coming from the cattle—now seemed commonplace and ordinary. Francis climbed up on a fencepost upwind and looped his legs through the slats. We kept regular time with Bosco who yelled that we only had about thirty head left. Dad uncovered his bucket and started back in with the scalpel, making steers out of bulls. When he cut the first scrotum and the balls plopped in the bucket, Francis said, "Ouch" and shook his head. I said, "We'll save you some for dinner" and Dad told me to shut up.

Every time I pulled on the lever, securing the steer, I felt like my head was going to explode. I held my breath while I pulled it down, using my whole body to back it up. There was pressure right behind my eyes. I felt like one of those *Loony Tunes* when Sylvester the cat has a hose stuck down his throat and his body gradually bloats, then flies off like a sputtering balloon. I was so concentrated on how shitty I felt that I started straining to keep up with the kick bar. One time, I misplaced the bar and the calf kicked it off. "What's the matter with you?" my dad said. "Stop acting like a fucking drunk." I wanted to say something, but I knew that it would get worse. I just swung the lever down, pulled the cradle shut, and locked the calf's head in place. I would've collapsed if I hadn't screwed up again. This time, I missed the kick bar altogether and the calf's legs were free and it kicked once, hard, sending me sprawling back. I picked myself up and limped back to the cradle, my eyes bloodshot, my Wranglers torn. "That's it." Dad snapped off his rubber gloves and handed them to me. Then he took my place, leaving me with the bucket of balls, the bloody scalpel, and the sterilizing solution.

No one could have predicted what happened next, although looking back it was the one singular moment that matched so much of the research we had done. Once DJ Tripp, alone in his booth, hallucinated that spider webs were enveloping his shoes. Another time, during a routine exam, he thought that his doctor was actually an undertaker about to bury him alive. The stories got worse when sleep deprivation was used as a form of torture. One was a sleep-deprived prisoner who had a cellmate who died after a week. At night the prisoner would see white snakes coming out of the floor. They would climb on his skin and bite him, leaving marks and injecting poison into his body. But then he'd look and his skin would be clear. His cellmate had it worse. He cowered and cried all the time, *no please God, they're eating me, they're eating me, make it stop, please, stop.* He punched the air, wailing and writhing. Then he would hit himself and claw at his face and roll up into the fetal position and a guard would come in and kick him awake. He'd kick and kick and the cellmate wouldn't move, but his eyes were open. The other guards had to come in and then there were people in and out constantly to make sure that the cellmate didn't succumb to sleep. When they thought he'd had enough, a doctor examined him and took his temperature and then they gave him a wool blanket and left the room. The prisoner touched his cellmate's skin and he was cold, ice-cold, even with the blanket, even after hours of sleep. The next day, the cellmate stopped breathing.

When the next calf came through, I found I couldn't move. The calf's sack swung back and forth like a pendulum and I held the scalpel with both hands. I thought, maybe if this was a wand, if it was longer, I could just wave it at the calf's scrotum and the testes would pop out. I tried to move my hand forward but it was like I was a body of phantom limbs; in my mind my arms were moving; I could see myself making the first incision, slicing from the perineum, and pulling out the testes into a bucket. I'd watched it happen so many times, the same movements over and over, but my body wouldn't follow through. Was I paralyzed? I started to panic, said "It's not working" a couple times until my dad said "Do it," forcefully, in a way that made me shift my eyes away from the pendulum swing of the calf's scrotum. Something had happened.

It was my dad. He looked horribly obese, with dark welts on his face like cigar burns. "Do it, now," he said. His mouth was rimmed with blood and his chin shook like a crying child's and testes dribbled out of his mouth in fluid like egg whites. I felt my muscles tense, the striations in my back growing tight the way they did before I braced for impact on the football field. I still held the scalpel in my two hands and my fingers curled around the metal shaft. The diseased dad took a tentative step toward me and his face grew more scarred, his flesh turning dark as loamy earth. Bits of flesh fell from his face like it was being chewed off. "You stay back," I said. I still couldn't move so I looked down into the big bucket of balls before me. There was part of my mind that knew what I was experiencing was irrational, a kind of detached consciousness that saw everything I was doing like a textbook on sleep deprivation. This was normal, I thought. I was hallucinating, nothing more. I could hear Parkins saying "What's wrong with him?" and my father's "Steady, steady" as he reached for my scalpel. I could see their confused faces and my taut body, still as a statue. But these images were equally blended with this new world, a heightened reality where I saw things as they truly were: my father, a decomposing man, Parkins hairy as a Neanderthal. I looked into the bucket now and saw not walnut-sized prairie oysters, but leeches, thick as my thumb, teeming, slick, in search of a host. Finally, my body responded. This was a dangerous place to be. I backed away, my hands out for balance like I was on the deck of a rocking ship. The scalpel gleamed in my right hand, ready to slice anything that came near. Parkins and my dad advanced on either side of the steer and Francis jumped down from the fence. He was the only one who still resembled himself. Same clothes, same scar splitting his lip. His hair was mussed and his face was dirty and streaked with sweat. But he was larger, almost colossal. His legs were muscled and his arms thick and sinewy. He said, "What's in the bucket, Darcy." He said it low, a statement, like he would rip my head open if I didn't tell. "Leeches," I said and I backed away further. Giant Francis picked up the bucket, said, "These are leeches?" and for a moment everything stopped, crisis averted. I wasn't pissed but crazy, and in response they all started to laugh. As they laughed, leeches began to appear in the eye sockets of my dad's decomposing face, crawling through the hair of Parkins' Neanderthal arms. Fluid from the hours of castration wriggled on the ground and snaked their way toward me. The leeches were everywhere, multiplying on their bodies like flies. I backed away, cowed, my scalpel the only thing threatening to cut through it all. And before anyone could stop him, Giant Francis grabbed the bottom of the bucket and slung all its contents, a long writhing arc of leeches, onto my body where they landed, sucked onto my skin like a million pinpricks and began to feast.

THE MAN WHO
LAUGHED HIS HEAD OFF

I'm in the garden talking to myself, a veritable Adam
without the Eve, naming roses as I plant them. That one
I'll call "wart-blossom." A rose by any other name, eh
Chuck? They're all the same flowers, purple-throated
hybrids. Kendra would like the purple. Purple, purple,
purple, I love *purple*. My ex-wife's favorite color, good ol'
Brenda, Glenda, Kendra. She hated it when I twisted her
name for the sounds. "They're not me," she'd say. "I'm
Kendra, your wife. Chuck . . ."

I'd needle her forever just to hear my name.

I feel like I'm planting weeds. Dunged up, the garden
could grow plenty of alfalfa. A whole forage crop. Mow it,
riding Thor, that's my mower. Or it is now. Willed to me
by my Uncle Parry with the cabin, the woods, the Alberta
wilderness, all part of the package. Who would've
guessed? The lucky recipient, a winning lottery number. A
rookie hockey card picked up by Antique Road show.
Oprah says there's unclaimed money out there. Piles of
cash, pieces of paper, deeds in your name. That's the
ticket, Chuck. Move out of Lethbridge's Tudor Estates so
that the gigolo can move in. Kendra won't have to lift a
finger. The gigolo's got money, religion. And Matt, Con-
nor, and Allie, my magnificent kids. One of those traveling
gigolos who'll give them presents. Origami dollar bills,
Pennants for Taylor. Plenty of plush.

Gardening can be art.

I once had an English teacher who wrote a sonnet every day. Italian, Petrarchan, Shakespearean, and then some combinations to keep himself from getting bored. He never read them to us. Just told us about them. Wanted to preserve the memory of his sonnet-writing more than the sonnets, so when the biographers showed up forty years later, they would talk to his students, his friends who knew him, then search his home for the thousands of sonnets and publish them posthumously. People would read them and find them meaningful, because, of course, he was a professor of English, and, of course, he died.

That's how I like to think of my gardening.

My cabin sits in a dimple between two foothills surrounded by evergreens. There is a lawn. It's been over a week since I got here, hauled my bare essentials in a trailer. That was a trip, Chuck. Never knew how far I'd pull off to the side of the road. In the ditch and out again, like the Dukes of Hazard. There's a story there. Heading down a hill like a grizzly's bearing down. That's the right verb, isn't it? Bearing kids. Bearing down, more than I can bear.

The flowerbed is a bean-shaped swimming pool. Two pitcher's mounds connected by mulch. A cell in the middle of meiosis. Five potted rose bushes at the center of each mound and I'm good to go. More hybrids. Purple and white and red all over.

Chuck, the phone is ringing. Chuck, go get it. It's your wife, Chuck. It has to be your wife. Damn it, I can't make out the words. At the end, it beeps.

The Parry Cabin is an encroachment. I've seen it with the forest pushed back, kids rushing unhinged from its doors. Plastic table cloths on picnic tables, a porch full of people. From the driveway, it was like a bourgeois sigh. And now. Well, things grow. Uncle Parry planted a Douglas Fir that obscures the sun. Inside, dishes pile up. My dishes, Chuck's dishes. Piled up after a week of precious solitude.

Who's idea was it to move out here anyway? It was mine, Chuck, all mine. You are here for good.

I play the message.

"Chuck, dear, Chuck, are you there?"

I'm here honey. I'm always here.

"Pick up if you're there. Matt's gone. He took the car. Have you seen him Chuck? He didn't come home, Chuck."

I go back to my gardening, and I bring out the cordless and put it in my mailbox. I pretend that the phone can hear me. Hello, phone. My alter ego. What do you say to a round of cards? Gardening's getting dull and my hands aren't used to the shape of a hoe. Hands full of blisters. What do you say? You've got some poker face. That's an advantage, phone. I'll never know what hit me. I plunge my trowel into a wheelbarrow full of dung.

Now that I'm a local, Waterton feels like a movie set. I go to Zum Burger Haus, a restaurant bar that serves burgers on Kaiser buns and has Heineken on tap. Tables made from hewn logs, the tops cross-sections from trees the size of Sequoias. Main Street is all t-shirts, waffle cones, and hiking boots. I find myself turning the corner, past the theatre, to the one hardware store in town. A monopoly. In the mountains, you can do that. Inside, I pretend to look at hoses. They have three kinds, one with a ten-year warranty. I like the idea of warranties.

The shopkeeper is a man my age with a moustache like a dead hamster. God, that's ugly, Chuck. Tawny, grey, and white and it's covering a harelip. He's got one hand on his utility belt. Only thing I can see on it is a tape measure. I notice that he's missing his left index finger. Just a small stump at the knuckle. What the hell, I think.

"Do you got any fencing?" I ask. Extend my left hand straight out. "I'm Chuck." Guy looks at my hand like it's got a disease. I'm sick of talking around people, and truth is, I want to know, so I say, "What happened to your hand?"

"Grain auger," he says. As if augers explain everything.

"Hell of a stump," I say. "I'd put some ice on that."

"I think you'd better leave," he says.

Damn it, Chuck, you're a dickhead. Two days of seclusion and look where it gets me. I take the hose up to the cash register. Stumpy takes his time, doesn't talk. I wonder if many tourists come in here.

The grass is always greener, my mother always said. The phone is still in the mailbox when I drive up and unload the hose. I don't even need a hose. Good move, Chuck. I wonder if this is how people go crazy. That's why I second guess myself when the phone rings. Twice in one day. Since I've been here, that's a record. I pick up this time, shoulder the hose.

"Chuck, did you get my message? Matt's gone. Did he phone you?"

"No."

"We have the police looking for him."

"The RCMP."

"They think he might be heading to see you."

Of course he's heading to see me. Mr. Gigolo is a weenie.

"That would be nice," I say.

Kendra says, "This is serious, Chuck. We're all very worried over here. He needs stability. If he contacts you, tell him that. Tell him we want to take care of him."

"I've been doing some gardening, Kendra. You'd like it here."

"I'm sure I would. You take it easy, Chuck. Remember what I said."

I don't hang up the phone. Chuck isn't ready to stop talking. There is something reasonable about Kendra's voice that I like. It sounds better than mine. I can hear what I say like an echo in the receiver. Different from the voice I talk to myself in. I don't hang up. I wait. I'm plugging the pause for drama.

"Kendra," I say. "I did something wrong, didn't I?"

"That's not something I want to talk about, Chuck. You want to place blame. I'm not going to let you."

"You should really come out here. Bring the kids. We'll have a barbecue."

"I *have* the barbecue, Chuck."

"Ever seen a rose with a purple throat?"

"Hang up the phone, Chuck."

Impulse tells me the phone is a dud. It's time to burn the thing, and I'm not talking displaced rage. How can a phone say words like that? Take it easy, Chuck. It's a phone, a phone. E.T. phone home. I decide to plant it. Cover the cordless with soil and mulch. And this is what I'm doing when Matt drives up and honks. Cheeky kid.

Slow motion here. This is how I picture it: Matt pulls the car into the driveway, opens the door and there's a close up on his boots, a pair of steel-toed Caterpillars. He steps out of the car and looks lovingly on his biological mess of a father who is crouched over a flowerbed planting a cordless phone deep into the earth. Their gazes lock; the son knows instantly the pain, the anguish, the loss, the hurt, the duress, the longing, the loneliness, the depravity, the self-loathing his father has been experiencing. He strides toward his father leaning forward with his hands lightly outstretched. There is an embrace and one or either or both of them are crying, sobbing wet globs of snot into each other's shoulders. They're shuddering, shaking, sharing the moment like emotional lunkheads, and they walk into the house arm in arm. Chuck, this is a flourish and you know it.

"Hey Dad," Matt says. "Could I use your phone?"

Matt looks the same as when I saw him last week. I even think they're the same clothes. I walk around and around him while he makes the call back to Kendra. The phone smells like earthworms and I'm glad that I didn't mangle it. "I wasn't going to let you just let him abandon himself out here," he says. I only get snippets of the conversation. He tells her outright that he's trying to convince me to move back to the city. So conscientious. He's a keeper, Chuck. At least there are some things I haven't fucked up.

"I'm not going back," I say when he gets off the phone.

"What are you doing out here, Dad? There's nothing here. It's in the middle of the woods. In the winter you won't even be able to *hike* here."

"Why did you run away? You know we've been worried. Your mom has been worried. You know that, don't you?"

"Sure, Dad, sure. Just take it easy, don't get all whacked out."

Matt puts the phone on the hook, picks up his duffel bag and takes it into the bedroom across from mine. He kicks a mound of laundry from the hallway into my room. Chuck, this house is a mess. I wander around the cabin, running my hands through my hair. I do this when I don't know what else to do. Now what? Chuck, there are things.

I phone Kendra when Matt is in the shower. The gigolo is there I can tell, huffing in the background. She's told me that the gigolo is moral, dependable. Predictable, I translate.

"I'm not coming back to town," I say.

"I didn't ask you to."

"You can call off the posse, now. Tell your gigolo he can stop pretending he's worried."

"He's not a gigolo."

"Matt came to see *me*," I say.

"He's not staying out there. If he doesn't leave by tomorrow, I promise that you'll never see him again."

Outside, I hook up the hose to the back spout, and pull it around the side of the cabin before I spot a bear in our front yard. A black bear, full grown, with its paws in my roses, digging like a dog planting a bone. No time to get crazy. I don't want to scare it off. I lay down the hose and walk to the front porch with my hands in my pockets, slow.

I have only seen a bear once before, after a ribbon of SUVs and station wagons on the road down from Redrock Canyon. It was up on a hill, lumbering through the spines of bear grass, crossing a clearing. Five cars on the shoulder, cameras and camcorders out the window. At one point, the bear stopped and sat on its haunches like a squirrel rotating a nut, watching the tourists in a row.

But this is the first time, close.

The bear sniffs, its brownish muzzle moving in an arc, leading it up facing me, then down, and away. I watch the black bulge of its haunches as it skirts the driveway, then heads into the trees. I listen.

"Dad?"

Matt will believe me, about the bear. I tell him when we park the truck near a wedge-shaped church just off Main Street.

"When you were in the shower," I say. "Just before you came out."

"There wasn't anything there, Dad. You're delusional. Why don't we just pack our stuff tonight?"

"We're celebrating. First night out with your dad."

Matt doesn't know this, but it is my goal to get him pissed drunk. He's sixteen, but looks twenty. With me he'll look even older. Chuck and upchuck. We get off Main Street and head to a local bar called the Thirsty Bear. No tourists.

I've seen this bar before it was a bar. They called it the Armory, but it was basically just a warehouse with a stage for shows on the weekends. The stage is still there, but the permanent tables and chairs, the rustic, rocky mountain décor fill it up, make it look stuffy. It's still early and we take a table over near the bar.

Before Matt can say anything, I've ordered us two beers.

There's a band doing a Crash Test Dummies cover, a sped-up "Superman." Now there's a song you can't forget. It'll stick, Chuck, forever. I sing along, "'The world will never see another man, like him.' Matt, you're not drinking?"

"You know I'm a minor."

"Drink up, Bud," I say.

I fiddle around with my beer. Somebody's going to have to drive us home, and it's not going to be me. Hell with it. I take Matt's drink and order him a Root Beer. This is when the hardware guy walks in, four-fingered hand behind a dumpy-looking blonde. He sits at the bar with his girl.

"Matt," I say, "how would you like to make fifty bucks?"

"I'm not going to drink, Dad."

"All you have to do is say something to a friend of mine."

"Why?"

"You see that guy over there? Just go up to him. Ask him if he isn't 'Stumpy' who owns the hardware store. But you have to say 'Stumpy' or it's a no-go."

"I don't think so, Dad."

"He's a friend of mine," I say. "It's a joke between us."

"Why the fifty bucks, then? What's the joke?"

Matt isn't budging and I'm not sure that I want him to. Some test of faith for the little bugger. But it doesn't matter because now Stumpy is looking my way. He's coming over.

"I don't think you should be here," he says.

I push back from the table a bit and hold my hands like I'm in a stickup. "I'm just having a drink here with my boy."

"This is a local bar," he says. "I'll give you a bit of time to get your stuff and go." The guy walks away.

"I am a local," I say. Only Matt can hear.

"I thought he was your friend," he says. I stay for a few minutes out of pure meanness. Truth is, I feel pathetic. I am "the ugly" in the good and the bad. And Matt keeps nagging for us to go home, to head back to the cabin. We leave the bar and go to Zum's.

Zum's isn't far from The Thirsty Bear, but it's fre-
quented entirely by tourists. People from all over Europe,
some Asians. Not hardly one damn Canadian. We stay for
a while and I try to get Matt to pick up a couple girls from
Montana. They wear long pants and new ropers. I can't
tell how old they are, but they're between Matt's and my
ages, so I figure that levels the playing field. But Matt's not
interested and the girls aren't buying. This makes me feel
very old.

When we get back into my Chevy, I see Stumpy and
his girl. They are on their way to a truck the size of a
house. Monster wheels. A regular show-stopper, Chuck.
Matt sees me watching them and I tell him to drive by.
"Drive by," I say. He drives by. Good kid. It's a show-
down, so I roll down my window. "Hey Stumpy," I say.
That's enough to get him chasing us.

This is where I'm trying to finish. The way my life has
been going, what Chuck wants, Chuck gets. And there's no
reason for him not to—not here. A violent ending, a
drunken ending. Say, a truck chase. Matt at the wheel,
winding through the foothills, Waterton behind them, a
scattershot of light. They're listening to music and trying to
outrun a Tonka truck with mammoth-sized wheels. There
will be a gun, a bear, a crash, tires spinning in new gravel,
a drive in the ditch, then up a ravine and through the front
doors of the Parry Cabin. That's high drama, Chuck, the
clincher. Maybe it should end in death? I remember my
mother's funeral two years ago. Kendra says I could still be
reeling from it. She used a persuasive metaphor I can
never forget. It wasn't ripples in the water or the domino
effect. She said some things happen to you like getting
sprayed by a skunk. You can bathe in tomato juice all you
want and you'll still smell like shit. Kendra didn't mince
words. Death, it could be. Like Mom. When she died, she
couldn't physically control what went in or out of her
body, but she still had her mind. Catheters everywhere.

Most people would get depressed by this. Maybe she was, but she didn't show it. The nurse would remove one bag of liquid feeding into her bloodstream, hook up another and my mother'd say, "Looks like it's time for dinner."

But during the chase, I see Matt wants it some other way. Matt looks in the rear view mirror and wiggles the wheel back and forth. There's a fair amount of play in there. His eyes focus on the two beads of light behind us. He's pleading, wondering what went wrong. He wants to pull over, let the monster truck fly by. Matt's drunk father will acquiesce, apologize. He'll tell Matt jokes. Like the one about the man who laughed his head off. That's a good one, Chuck. Hah hah hah, thump thump thump. What's that sound? A man laughing his head off. "You're such a moron," he'll say and then laugh with his dad. Matt wants Yogi and Booboo stories in the dark, barbecues with his father wearing a white mushroom hat. He wants dates and nostalgia. Matt remembers his father siphoning gas from one car to the next, because one had broken down and the other was empty, the gas station closed, just so Matt wouldn't miss a date with Darla. He smells Chuck's gasoline breath. He sees the marks the hose made around his mouth. Suck it up, Chuck. Suck it up.

A wink or a nudge could do it, Chuck. A flourish—a tap on the brakes to stop the truck, to stop the words from bearing down.

SEVEN LITTLE STORIES ABOUT SEX

The boy's first French kiss was with a teddy bear. Her name was Melissa. She had blue fur, like shag carpet, two dimples for eyes, and a plastic one-piece nose and mouth. His brother told him, this is how it's done. You put your tongue in their mouth and move it around. You need to know how to do it right when you get a girl. So the boy held Melissa's head with both hands and licked the plastic slot that was Melissa's mouth. His tongue dipped down like a hummingbird darting into the throat of a flower, slurping up nectar.

* * *

Every month, the boy had an interview with his father. His father wrote down their conversation and made a list of goals to accomplish. The father wrote, "Have homework done every day by five. Get above 90% on the next math test." And always, "Read the Bible."

Once, the boy's father talked about being in graduate school. He opened one of his mile-thick textbooks filled with diagrams and equations. His father had a pad of paper on his knees and he drew what looked like a sports play, with arrows and circles and squiggly lines. The boy moved his chair so he was looking at the shapes from the same angle. His father wrote "MEIOSIS" in block letters, then "WOMAN" next to a large round circle and "MAN" next to one of the squiggly lines. Then "SPERM" and "EGG." He wrote these down in no apparent order and then he described the flagellating sperm swimming up a woman's fallopian tubes to penetrate the egg. The boy's father used many words that the boy didn't know: mitochondria, flagellum, TK inhibitors, implantation, zygote. The father drew more pictures: the egg halved, then quartered, then grew into a bunch like grapes or a cluster of frog eggs. The boy understood that this was how every human being started, the proliferation of two cells dividing. But the father forgot to explain the sex part, how the sperm and the egg got to be in the same place at the same time and so for years the boy thought the sperm flew out of the man and through the air to where it entered the woman and multiplied like cancer.

* * *

Once the boy was on a playground. The playground had see-saws and monkey bars and a metal dome of welded triangles. The boy rode a donkey on a giant spring next to a plastic turtle. He was waiting for his mother to meet him halfway from school, like she usually did, sauntering up in overalls and sandals, her hair in a bun. Three teenage boys with black or grey t-shirts came up to him. They had chains on their pockets and their pants hung so low that their crotches were almost down to their knees. Their hair was long and un-parted.

"Do you want to see a lizard?" one of them asked.

The boy said yes. He liked lizards. He knew that their ancestors were dinosaurs and lizards reminded him of these great ancestors, their regal heads and their bones in the Tyrell museum that he had been to with his class. Yes, he wanted to see a lizard. They were rare in Alberta; in fact, he couldn't remember ever seeing one out in the wild—only in interpretive centers or zoos.

The middle teenager, the one with a silver loop splitting his bottom lip, pointed to a plastic turtle, said, "I saw a lizard go under that turtle."

The boy got off the donkey and climbed down to look. There was about a half-foot space between the gravel and the turtle, so the boy pushed some of the gravel out of the way with his hand. The teenager said, "That's right, go all the way under and you'll see it." The boy did as he was told and went in under the turtle. He could sit up now. The turtle's plastic shell diffused the light, making everything a pale green. "I don't see it," the boy said. The teenagers were laughing. "Keep looking." The boy said, "I can't see it anywhere!" The teenagers threw rocks at the shell and the rocks made a sound like knuckles rapping a table. One said, "It's out here now. Come quick!" The boy climbed out and the sun seemed brighter than before and he looked at the feet of the boys to see if there was a lizard winding its way through the gravel, camouflaged like a chameleon or a green anole, blending into the smoky rocks. But there was no lizard, only one of the boys with his pants even lower, and a penis hanging out of his boxers, limp and hairy. "There's your lizard," the teenager shouted before pulling his pants back up, a now-you-see-it, now-you-don't trick, and they were off just as the boy saw his mother running toward them, angry-looking, her sandals thwacking her heels, and the boy thought, that was not a lizard, that was definitely *not* a lizard.

* * *

Grade seven, the boy took the bus to middle school. The boy's family moved to the United States and the boy had started to learn to play the violin. The school put him in EEO: Extended Educational Opportunities. The boy still spoke Canadian; he said serviette for napkin, chesterfield for couch. Initially the boy was shy for saying these words, was embarrassed when kids would introduce him to other kids, like he was some Canadian ambassador. Two girls took it upon themselves to make him a badass. The boy had never been a badass before. One of the girls took the same bus to school. She sat one row in front of him and turned around in her seat and laid her head on her hands and asked him what it was like to live in Canada.

The boy said, "It's colder."

The girl said, "How cold?"

The boy said, "Colder than here." Then they stopped talking.

"We are going to make you into such a badass," the girl said.

The boy didn't know why, but talking to the girl was hard for him. And exciting. He had bought the jeans that the girl told him about, the ones that she said made his ass look great. He felt that this was important: a good ass to be a badass. He was glad for the jeans, too, because they were loose and when he sat down, the crotch bunched up in the front so that there was plenty of room if he got an erection. He got erections all the time now, whenever the two girls would grab him by the hands and take him to their lockers or when they hugged him between classes and he could feel their incipient breasts against his chest. And the morning. The morning on the bus was the worst. He was tired and groggy and just the vibration of the bus would set it off. That's why, when he talked to the girl, he couldn't say much. He was wondering if she could see his erection in the folds of his loose pants, the pants that she told him to buy, the good-ass pants.

But now they were at the school and the kids were getting off the bus, shuffling past one another, wires trailing from ears into pockets, backpacks swinging, and the girl was waiting for the boy and the boy said, "I'll be there in a second," because he was at full mast now and the lack of vibration wasn't doing squat. So he picked up his violin case from where it lay at his feet. It was hard and black and plastic, shaped a little, he thought, like a penis. He

held the case in front of him so that it angled up, a giant
erection hiding his little one. The girl was ahead of him
now and the case bumped against his good-ass jeans until
he could feel the swelling starting to work its way out, and
then they were moving through the glass double doors and
the girl was waving to her friend and she took the boy by
the hand and twirled and twirled him so that the other girl
could see how good he looked in his new jeans.

* * *

Yanking your Yoda. The new *Star Wars* had just come
out and the boy made a fist and unclenched and held his
limp penis in his hand. Poor Yoda, about to be strangled.
To be a Jedi, strangle him you must.

The boy made up the phrase at a friend's house. They
found a colloquial dictionary that the boys took turns reading. Masturbation wasn't something the boy felt comfortable discussing openly; for all he knew, he was the only
one of his friends who yanked his Yoda day after day. But
reading the various euphemisms was somehow OK: bop-
ping the bishop, choking the chicken, beating the meat,
spanking the monkey, feeding the geese, yanking the
chain, stroking the salami. The boys were prudish, came
from prudish families, which made the words hilarious.
Passing the book around was like what the boy imagined
sharing a joint or a bottle of Tequila might be like, each
new euphemism adding to their mutual intoxication.

But now the boy stood in front of his mirror and he felt
a sickly guilt for the words: pounding the midget, spanking
the plank, burping the worm, milking the lizard, doing the
five-knuckle shuffle, cleaning the pipes, flogging the dol-
phin, punching the clown, siphoning the python, jerking
the gherkin. The boy hoped the words would bring back
that feeling of clutching his stomach, his breaths short and
shallow, water in the corner of his eyes. Only Yoda made
him smile now. There was something about the shape of

his Jedi head, the peaked dome of it, the foreskin-like wrinkles on his face and his wispy curls like pubic hair that made the boy laugh so hard his abdomen was sore. The boy's priest had told him, warned him about his sin, the sin of Onan, self-abuse, masturbation. There were consequences. Think of every sperm as the potential for life, he said. Millions of lives wasted on the ground, spilled. Would he want those lives on his hands? Those unborn souls chasing him through eternity? It would drive him mad in the afterlife, would be like being boiled alive in his own sperm. *Boiled alive.*

The boy thought back to the first time he had jerked his gherkin. He was young, eleven or twelve maybe, his penis not fully grown. It was at night, on the waterbed that he shared with his kid brother. He had trouble sleeping, would diddle with himself out of comfort, to help the sleep come on. He remembered the feeling the first time, a great whoosh of energy from his groin permeating his body. Nothing came out at first, no dead sperm, no souls chasing him through eternity. But gradually they came, every night, day after day, his seminal volume growing as he developed. Soon he was spurting, had to bring a towel to bed to clean up as inconspicuously as possible, the millions of sperm rising to the top, following each other up and out, like lemmings diving off a cliff. Now he was in high school, was jerking off a couple of times a day, each couple spurts adding to the vat of sperm waiting for him in the afterlife. He tried to fix this image in his mind: A huge cauldron, like the ones used in Disney cartoons, a witch's brew where flames licked the sides and him roasting in there like a boiled cabbage. His penis wasn't limp anymore but slightly engorged. He thought of the heat, searing heat, and his face melting like wax. His penis grew harder. The vat of semen was on fire, the flames engulfing, charring his face, and he smelled burning flesh. He was hard as a steel rod now and slowly, in spite of himself, his hand started to pump, yanking Yoda from his grave as the vat and all its contents went white hot and he felt himself, just for an instant, lifted away.

* * *

At college, late at night, the boy and his girl made lazy figure-eights down landscaped medians on the way to the cathedral at the center of town. They were barely eighteen, under-aged drinkers nursing their buzz with rum and Cokes. The cathedral was near the top of a hill and the boy led her around behind. He had a Navaho blanket and she wore a spaghetti-strapped top and a pair of khaki shorts that barely covered her buttocks. Behind the cathedral was a park with grass and a spectacular view and it was three o'clock in the morning and they had been talking about how they could spend all night together and all of the next day and the next and not tire of each other's company and wasn't that unique and great? So much more freedom than either of them had had growing up. The boy put the blanket down like he was laying a bedspread and he propped himself up on one elbow with the girl still standing and he was thinking how good she looked with the lights of the cathedral behind her and her soft cream legs and the spot on her back right above her buttocks which was the only place she had allowed him to touch freely since they had been dating these two months.

The girl lay down beside him, facing him, and she said, "What are you thinking?" Always the same question whenever they were close.

He wanted to say thinking of putting his hand between her legs because his friend Travis said that's how to get a girl hot but instead he said, just how great it would be to be with you forever and the girl said that she'd been thinking the same thing. And then she looked down at the cathedral, its white lights shining up to its spires and arches, and he realized she was thinking the M-word and he was thinking sex and he wondered if talking about the

M-word could get him sex if he was careful. He liked this girl, he really did, but he had a condom in his back pocket and Travis had been razzing him for a week that it had taken him so long to score.

"Here," the boy said. "You look cold."

He pulled the edge of the Navaho blanket over her and then he rolled her toward him so that she was lying comfortably in his arms and he pulled the other end of the blanket around him so they were like two larvae inside a cocoon. She put his arm around her and placed it on her stomach.

"I feel so safe with you," she said.

His hand felt like it was on fire. He had a vague idea of what was below her navel, that there was hair and a hole and labia and moisture and so he rubbed her belly and put his index finger in her navel and wiggled it around some. Then, as if it were a power button turning her on, she rotated toward him and placed her hand on his cheek and opened her mouth to him. He moved his lips and let his tongue do some of the work and he tried to move his head around and brush his fingers lightly against her face like he'd seen actors do in movies. He put his hand on her shoulder blades and massaged where it met her side, just under her armpit and he slowly slid his hand over with each combination of kisses. But as soon as he felt the padded cup of her bra, she took his hand and put it on her thigh and then she rolled on top of him.

The boy was a little timid now—he didn't want to put his hands where they weren't wanted—but the girl was kissing him more earnestly and she had done a strange thing with her legs. They were parted over his upper thigh and as she kissed him, she pressed against him and she kissed him more quickly. He eased his thigh up against her crotch and her body became taut, like a tuned string. She moved faster now and his hand was on the back of her jeans and she pulled her face away from his so that she could breathe. He wanted her now, wanted every part of himself inside her and he saw on her face not desire but a look of confusion or surprise, her eyes open so that he could see the milky whites even with just the low light of the cathedral behind her. Her hair hung down and a few strands were wet and caught against the side of her face like the loop of a question mark.

Then he stopped. Abruptly he stopped. There was a fire-fly-sized light directly to the side of him that shook and flickered as it approached. The boy stopped and the girl smoothed his face with her hand and said, "What's wrong?" And he said, "Shhh." She rubbed his chest and bent down to kiss him and she squeezed his thigh with her legs.

"I think there's a guy coming," he said.

She untangled her legs and slid down alongside him and put her head on his chest just as the light licked the edges of the Navajo blanket and dazzled their eyes. "Sorry to bother you," the man said. "I'm going to have to ask you to move." He was gone almost as quickly as he came. He explained how it looked. The church didn't like people making out on the lawn.

Back on the median, on the way to their dorm rooms, the boy and his girl wrapped the blanket around themselves like they were a couple of refugees. It was a while before either of them spoke. The boy was embarrassed and still incredibly horny but the girl shrugged him off every time.

Finally, she said, "We just had sex with our clothes on." It was like the finger of God had come down and named it.

But the boy said, "I don't think so."

* * *

The boy, married, seven years last April. He was lying in bed depressed. His wife lay on her side with her hand on his chest. They had failed their first round of in vitro fertilization last month and they had two embryos in storage for the next. So here they were, the failed parents, in the eye of the storm, two weeks after his wife's period, waiting.

The boy remembered last month, the nights where he gave his wife progesterone shots. He would swab the bit of skin behind her hip bone with rubbing alcohol and push a needle through the fatty tissue and into the muscle. His wife sucked air through her teeth. Sometimes it hurt more than others. What did it feel like? There were little red pricks all over her hip after a full month of injections. Gave another meaning to needling your wife. The boy needled her every night, "shooting up" they called it, all because the boy had problems, below-the-belt problems, whirligig sperm and too few of them.

Now, in bed, depressed, the boy thought of Dr. Zimmerman during their first meeting, before they signed the papers and froze the sperm and bought the progesterone-in-oil injections and shot up night after night.

First, the pitch: a story that Dr. Z had probably told to hundreds of aspiring parents but was new to the boy and his wife. "You don't have a lot of good-quality sperm," he said. Then he used a persuasive metaphor, a metaphor that the boy never forgot and then repeated word for word to his family, to his close friends, to some of his co-workers who tittered when they heard the word sperm: You are like a one-man army trying to invade China. Sure, there is the theoretical possibility that you'll be successful, but you would have a lot better chance if you had a whole army.

Then the stories.

The first was a couple in their forties and a man with a zero-sperm count. "Zero," Dr. Z said. They did a sperm extraction directly from the testes and came up with five blobs of bio matter that may have been healthy sperm at some point. They injected these into the woman's eggs and surprise! Produced two embryos. They transferred both and the woman got pregnant, gave birth to a baby boy. "The closest thing I've ever seen to immaculate conception," Dr. Z. said.

The second was less optimistic. In this one, a woman was gifted with multiple eggs, a whole farm of them, extracted from her ovaries by the dozens, the Follistim hormones doing their job. Her partner had several good sperm injected one by one into the eggs, fifteen healthy grade-A embryos, three transferred for good measure, the others frozen, and not a single take. They did it again and again, month after month and gave up after the money ran out. So, there's a spectrum of failure and success.

But for the boy and his wife, everything had been about average, middle of the bell curve. How many eggs? 10, about average. How many embryos? 5, about average. They had a forty percent chance, he knew, about average, for getting pregnant. This had made them hopeful. When his wife had her period the next month, he took a drive out into the country in the middle of a thunderstorm and cried, dripping tears and snot onto the steering wheel. Now they had another month to wait before trying again, another couple embryos on ice.

Lying there, the boy wondered if his wife was sleeping or deep in thought, dreaming perhaps like he often did about their unborn children. The idea of a child was still very abstract to the boy; he'd dreamed about his wife's growing abdomen, ultrasounds with bat-winged fetuses, or premature deaths. She birthed a tow-headed winged angel, triplet boys, a body-snatcher seed pod, and once, a Popple covered in green goo.

So the boy was surprised when his wife turned and put her hand on his chest and played with the hair there. Her hands were warm, supple, like the hands of a child. She touched his stomach and the boy could feel the familiar pull in his groin, that tingling in his penis as it became engorged with blood. He wasn't sure he wanted this. There was something sad about it, desperate, like a one-night stand or a truth-and-dare game. She touched him now in earnest and he felt his hardness in her hand.

The boy was still reluctant. Sometimes when the boy was very turned on he thought of calamities like burning houses or muzzled terriers in animal shelters or dentists giving root canals to try and push his mind from the sex, so it would delay his orgasm until his wife was coming so long and loud that it was all he could do to keep from giving in.

Tonight, he thought, dead baby, dead baby, dead baby. He started to go partly limp, like a wilted carrot. His wife pumped him for a while. Dead babies in burn barrels, dead babies in gutters, nannies pushing dead babies in strollers. His wife shifted in bed, went down and kissed him from his shaft to his glans. Her entreaties were so sincere, so tender that he found himself following her lead, moving the way she wanted him to in spite of the images he had conjured in his mind. The boy heaped all the dead babies into a mound, one for every one of his whirligig sperm, mouths agape, frozen in anguish, then pushed them away until they disappeared in a pinprick on the horizon of his mind. He let her pull him in on top of her and she came quickly and the boy moved, rocking and rhythmic, a man trying his best to give a woman a gift. She put her hands on his buttocks and he pushed in deeper and the woman groaned and said "Oh, oh." There was a feeling of possibility and sadness to their sex. How many times had they both let themselves be duped? A couple of infertile adults, humping like rabbits to try and prevent their own extinction. The boy pushed harder, the woman groaned softly, gulping breaths of air. Infertile adults, just a couple of oversexed and baby-less yuppies in their empty home with their empty cars, walking clichés, really, humping in futility. The boy thought, Baby Gap, pastel blues and pinks, car seats, nursing bras, mobiles, Gerber, nipples sore from teething, all images in miniature like a diorama of the first two years of life. He kept these in his mind until he was groaning too and he felt his body go tight and warm for a few moments and then slack. He lay on top of his wife, propped up slightly by his arms, not wanting to leave that place inside her. But she was crying. The boy moved, shocked by his wife's depth of feeling, his wife who never cried, who only said I love you if he said it first.

His wife touched his shoulder, almost pawing at it, while she wept.

And as he lay there, the boy confused yet happy, he thought how Dr. Z got it wrong. He imagined his sperm mixing with his wife's cervical mucus, struggling into her and swimming through the uterus. Over the next day millions of sperm would die, a literal genocide of his own genetic code. But one sperm would make it up to the ampullary portion of his wife's fallopian tubes where it would meet an egg, a full round egg in a nimbus of light. And that egg, in a process that nobody quite understands, would invite that one exhausted spermatozoon in, not like a warrior bent on invading China all by himself, but like a meeting between two wounded travelers, two souls who had been alone for so long, wanting to share some news, a chain letter telling the endless story of themselves, saying look, look how far we have come.

About the Author

Eric Freeze was born in Saskatoon, Saskatchewan and raised in southern Alberta. His stories, essays, and translations have appeared in a number of journals, including *Boston Review, The Southern Review, Prairie Fire, The Fiddlehead, Tampa Review, The Harvard Review* and *New Ohio Review.* He currently teaches creative writing at Wabash College in Indiana where he lives with his spouse and three young children.